SHERLOCK HOLMES

The Lone Rider

Christopher D. Abbott

Copyright © 2023 Christopher D. Abbott

Edited by Scott Pearson
SCOTT-PEARSON.COM

All rights reserved.
ISBN: 9798862378016 – ISBN: 9798852640406 (pbk.)

CDANABBOTT.COM

First Edition

For
John & Jeffrey

With special thanks to Scott Pearson, Richard Sutton, and Rob Reddan.

This is a work of fiction. Names, characters, places, and incidents are products of the author's imagination or are used fictitiously and are not to be construed as real. Any resemblance to actual events, locales, organisations, or persons, living or dead, is entirely coincidental.

Other Titles

MYSTERY: THE DIES SERIES
Sir Laurence Dies
Dr. Chandrix Dies

MYSTERY: THE WATSON CHRONICLES
SHERLOCK HOLMES: *A Scandalous Affair*
SHERLOCK HOLMES: *The Curse of Pharaoh*
SHERLOCK HOLMES: *The Langsdale House Mystery*
SHERLOCK HOLMES: *The Black Lantern*
SHERLOCK HOLMES: *Broken Glass*
SHERLOCK HOLMES: *Mystery at Granholm Asylum*
SHERLOCK HOLMES: *The Second Door*
SHERLOCK HOLMES: *Midnight Fire*
SHERLOCK HOLMES: *Cases by Candlelight*
SHERLOCK HOLMES: *The Tiger's Claws*
SHERLOCK HOLMES: *The King's Diamond*
SHERLOCK HOLMES: *Her Missing Red Pin*
SHERLOCK HOLMES: *Cases by Candlelight Vol.2*
SHERLOCK HOLMES: *The Haunted Mansion*
SHERLOCK HOLMES: *The Lone Rider*
SHERLOCK HOLMES: *Four Calling Birds*

FANTASY: THE SONGS OF THE OSIRIAN SERIES
Songs of the Osirian [Book 1]
Rise of the Jackal King [Book 2]
Daughter of Ra [Book 3]
Citadel of Ra [Book 4]
Songs of the Osirian: Companion

SUPERNATURAL/HORROR
Progenitor

CONTENTS

Other Titles

Introduction	2
Chapter One	4
Chapter Two	14
Chapter Three	27
Chapter Four	40
Chapter Five	54
Chapter Six	66
Chapter Seven	81
Chapter Eight	90
Chapter Nine	100
Chapter Ten	109
Epilogue	124
About the Author	130

SHERLOCK HOLMES

The Lone Rider

Introduction

I have been to the United States of America several times. It is a country both Holmes and I enjoyed travelling to and spending many weeks exploring. Our travels have taken us to St. Paul in Minnesota, where we had the pleasure of exploring the midwestern frontier on a very difficult case. We also spent time in Colorado, Detroit, California, and New York – but of *all* those cities and places travelled, New York still remains my favourite.

I've been back several times over the years. The city of New York is entirely different now, but if one is observant, however, it's possible to find places in that vast city that *still* invoke the spirit of those earlier horse-drawn days.

My eldest son, who is studying for his medical doctorate, plans to spend time in New York. The world changed dramatically after the War, and nearly every country who partook had its share of losses. And perhaps that's why I think this case came to mind.

When I explained to my sons their father *and* godfather were at the unveiling of the Statue of Liberty, they begged me to tell the story. I retrieved my notes and read through them, adding small details here and there that I could recall which added to their excitement.

'You should publish it,' my wife declared. 'The anniversary is coming up. Forty years.'

'Forty?' I said, chuckling. 'Forty years! It feels just like yesterday.'

John H. Watson, MD (Retd)
28th October 1926

Chapter One

The man you describe has been following us since we left the ship.

I suppose it was when I got my first sight of an American coastline that my excitement for our holiday really manifested. Our voyage had sadly been hampered by bad weather for several days, and even though I was used to rough seas, after a day or so, my tolerance lessened. It helped that I could offer my services as a doctor to anyone unwell, and it also helped that the crew of RMS *Germanic* did everything they could to make us comfortable. When our ship finally manoeuvred its way towards the New York harbour – and the rain had stopped long enough to be above deck – Sherlock Holmes joined me in the early-morning Autumn sea air for a smoke.

'We're about to witness a significant moment of history, Watson,' Holmes said, flicking his dying cigarette into the Atlantic. 'I would like you to keep notes of our activities.'

I nodded. 'I have always done so.'

My friend leant against the railing. 'We should arrive at the New York Harbour port in approximately two hours.'

'I admit I am very excited.'

Holmes turned a smile on me. 'My trips to the Americas are always a delight' – it was rare for me to hear Holmes wax lyrical with such conviction, and dare I suggest it... emotional sentiment? He must have read my thoughts because he straightened quickly beside me – 'and not in a mawkish or romantic way, you understand.'

'Oh, yes, I quite understand,' I fumbled. It didn't appear to abate his hard look.

I could already feel the ship changing direction, as Holmes looked to the sharpening coastline. He thrust out his long arm and pointed at a buoy. 'That's the harbour's first marker. We'll turn and find a place in the port lane now.'

I knew all of this already, but said nothing as Holmes – being the thorough man that he was – continued to school me on the differences between British and American maritime practices. Eventually, the conversation turned to our purpose in coming: the official unveiling of a statue named Liberty.

'It's the Statue *of* Liberty, Watson,' Holmes corrected. 'Not a statue *called* Liberty.'

'I understand they made it in France?'

Holmes nodded. 'Shipped block-by-block and assembled on her own island. The French refer to her as *La Liberté éclairant le monde*!'

'Liberty Enlightening the World?' I translated.

Holmes nodded. 'It was Édouard René Lefèbvre de Laboulaye who originated the idea, later turned into reality by the sculptor Frédéric Auguste Bartholdi. Edouard didn't live long enough to see its unveiling and dedication, sadly.'

'You knew him?'

'Yes,' my friend acknowledged, 'I admired his principles, if you will. He was a careful observer of the United States and an admirer of its constitution. He also wrote several volumes on American political history. I had the good fortune, one afternoon in Paris, to have spent several hours in his company. It really was a loss to the world when he passed away.'

My eyes fixed on the horizon as the ship slowly turned and followed the line to the harbour. Even though the wind had turned the light rain almost horizontal, we remained for an hour more. Holmes continually pointing out the various structures of interest. When we felt those giant engines reverse beneath us, shaking the ship as they slowed our momentum, we headed to our cabins to begin the disembarkation process.

Several hours later on a mid-morning Thursday of the 14th October 1886, Holmes and I stood patiently in line with the other first-class passengers, at the New York Port of Entry. Once we'd passed through, we met our contact at the Franco-American Union – an organisation who'd previously hired Holmes to investigate an affair of national importance, all of which I am told the word is not yet ready to hear – who greeted us and treated us both like royalty, from that moment on.

* * *

We arrived at the luxurious Fifth Avenue Hotel around three in the afternoon, and its architecture immediately impressed me. The building, constructed of brick and white marble, was of a plain Italianate style palazzo-front design, with a projecting tin cornice, but its sober exterior paled in comparison with its richly appointed interior of crimson and green curtains, suites of rosewood furniture with brocatelle marble tops, stunning carpets, and gilt wood as far as the eye could see. The entire hotel presented about as handsome and as comfortable an appearance as anyone need wish for and – in our case – everything we would ever need call for, since we were provided a suite of three rooms, at no expense to us. I had only seen such luxurious surroundings in a hotel once before in Paris, and the Fifth Avenue Hotel was on par with it.

While the porters unpacked our cases, the hotel treated us to a bottle of Dom Perignon Brut Champagne and oysters in a private dining suite reserved for only a very few people. Sherlock Holmes had been quietly observing everyone in the room whilst he sipped his drink, which he eventually replaced with his pipe.

'We have found ourselves in more luxury than I'd have

ever thought possible,' I whispered. 'More so than the first-class cabins on the ship, and that is saying something!'

'Yes, these fellows do like to make it known they have money,' Holmes said, lifting the bottle to refill our glasses. '1884,' he said, smiling. 'Not a terrible year.'

I also chuckled. 'Here's to our American adventure,' I toasted.

The dedication ceremony wasn't scheduled to occur until Thursday the 28th of October, and as we'd arrived a couple of weeks before that, there was time for an excursion or two. I sat in a private alcove across from the bar flicking through various flyers I'd collected for ideas to present to Holmes as our first expedition, and Maximillian's Park of Amusements immediately caught my eye. It was a new park with a train on a track called a rollercoaster, and I was just reading the details when an odd-looking fellow with short, messy greying hair, pasty skin, penetrating brown eyes, and a shuffling gait, had the impertinence to sit himself opposite me without bothering to ask if it was free. What was worse, he didn't seem interested in me at all. The side of the chair gave him cover to peer around at the bar, and when sense finally hit me, I protested his intrusion, and the fellow immediately stood, made a mumbled apology, and darted away before I knew what had happened.

'What is it, Watson?' Holmes asked when he appeared a moment later and took the chair.

I explained what had occurred whilst Holmes smoked his pipe and listened. When he asked me to re-tell it, I knew there was more going on. My friend considered me for a moment, then he slowly pushed his hand into the left side of his chair, past the cushion, and smiled. When his hand retracted, there was a small card in his slender fingers.

'Interesting,' Holmes said, examining the card. 'Did this fellow have a lameness in his left leg?'

I admit the question not only surprised me, but confounded me. 'How could you possibly know that?' I asked, far louder than I wanted to. Then I stared at the card in his hand and shook my head in wonder. 'You deduced it from that card?'

Holmes gave me an amused look, then said, 'Don't be ridiculous, Watson. The man you describe has been following us since we left the ship.' He held the card to his eyes. 'And it seems all he intended to do was deliver this.'

'What is it?'

'The business card of Thomas Henry Franke of Franke & Co. Pharmacy,' he said, turning it over. 'Well, well. How peculiar.'

'Peculiar fits this chap.' I chuckled.

Holmes tapped the card to his lips. 'Clearly, the fellow wishes to gain my attention, but his method is the peculiar point. You say he was peering over at the bar when he sat?' Holmes asked, sliding himself into the side of the chair. 'Like this?'

'That's right. I thought he was simply being rude.'

'Perhaps not. This fellow, did he seem furtive or scared?'

I replayed the encounter in my mind. 'Furtive, I think. I can't be entirely sure.'

'And it didn't appear to you as though he might fear being caught?'

'Possibly. I really wasn't paying that much attention.'

'It is a pity you didn't,' Holmes said, glancing at the bar. He then smiled. 'Can I refresh your drink, Watson?'

Sherlock Holmes spent several minutes at the bar in conversation with the barman, and those who'd flocked around him. It seemed his banter was appreciated, and by the sound of the rambunctious laughter these New Yorkers were prone to express, he had made several new contacts – for Holmes did nothing without gaining some advantage, or some fact, and would certainly not engage in idle chat at a bar for any other reason. When my friend returned and handed me my drink, he had a look in his eyes that said he'd uncovered something of value.

'What did you learn?'

'Not here,' Holmes muttered, sipping his whiskey soda. He seemed concerned someone might overhear us. 'Since it is a glorious day, let's finish these drinks and take a stroll along Fifth Avenue.'

Fifteen minutes later, we slowly meandered along the vast avenue, where light traffic passed infrequently.

Holmes pointed to a poster sign for a railroad. 'The Vanderbilt family,' he said, 'who found their success in the shipping and railroad empires of Cornelius Vanderbilt, owns a significant amount of Fifth Avenue. I'm told the ten blocks south of Central Park at Fifty-Ninth Street are known as Vanderbilt Row.'

'Told by who?'

'The porters at the hotel,' Holmes replied. 'These fellows know everything that happens between here and the adjacent streets and avenues, Watson. They know every other hotel, every porter, every scrap of street gossip, and they have connections *inside* those connections. We should be lucky to have a network like that. And yet they're a completely underused resource. The chief of the New York Police should be ashamed. Ah,' he said, stopping and pointing at the store sign he'd led us to. 'Here we are.'

It read: *Franke & Co., Pharmacy.*

Holmes held open the door and followed me in. There were customers, so we stood to one side examining racks of products. My friend held the curved handle of his cane in his gloved hand and watched it swing while we waited for the proprietor to finish assisting an attractive, regal-looking woman and her maid. There was an issue with a prescription he'd filled earlier. From what I overheard he'd made a mistake and then made a similar one soon after. It caused her a degree of agitation he quickly eased, and once her issues were resolved she headed for the door where I quickly intervened and held it open. She gave me a polite incline of her head and a smile I'd remember for several days after.

'Most kind, sir,' she said, leading her young maid away from the pharmacy. When I re-entered, Holmes was engaged in a conversation with the very fellow I'd seen earlier at the hotel. I suppose I should have considered he might have been the owner of that business card. I assumed he was simply a messenger.

As I approached, Holmes purchased a remedy for an earache that I could easily have made up for him, and then shook Mr Franke by the hand.

'Do nothing further until you hear from me,' my friend commanded.

'Understood, Mr Holmes,' Mr Franke said.

I tipped my hat at his smile, then my friend gestured to the door, and without further comment we left the pharmacy and made a slow journey back along Fifth Avenue, where Holmes explained what he'd learnt.

'The crux of the matter is simple. Around three days ago, the brother of Mr Franke disappeared under peculiar and mysterious circumstances.'

'How intriguing,' I said. 'And he wants you to investigate it?'

'He does,' Holmes said, directing us to a bench where we sat and each lit a cigarette. 'The circumstances are unique,' he remarked excitedly. 'Apparently, his brother, Henry Franke, came down from his bedroom to collect the morning paper, as he always did. It was during an animated conversation with his wife – who was in her bedroom on the floor above and therefore did not see what occurred – that he abruptly ceased talking. His wife then heard a clattering, and when she came to investigate, found his pyjamas and slippers in a pile, along with an opened newspaper and an upturned post tray on the floor, but of Henry Franke there was no sign. According to Mrs Franke, he'd vanished into thin air.'

'Impossible,' I laughed.

'That may be so, but it *is* an intriguing puzzle,' Holmes said.

A thought then occurred to me. 'How did Mr Franke know of you?'

'You don't think my name has reached the Americas?' Holmes asked.

'I did not think a pharmacist in New York would know it,' I admitted.

Sherlock Holmes reached into his pocket and presented me with a small four-page booklet printed for the statue unveiling. On it, amongst other advertisements, was a detailed schedule and list of well-known people in attendance, ranging from American government officials, and their many international counterparts, to a list of the very rich and famous families, including the Vanderbilts, along with dignitaries from other countries, including, 'Mr Sherlock Holmes, world-renowned detective from London, England, and his friend, Doctor John H Watson,' I read aloud.

'This brochure told Mr Franke we were coming. Thanks are due to you also, albeit to a lesser degree—' He must have seen the frown cross my face because he added, 'Franke has read several of those deplorable accounts of my work. He's an intelligent fellow, but limited. Once he'd tracked down our ship and learnt when we were due to land, he came to greet us before we left the harbour, but our contact took us directly to the hotel. The security is stringent, but has its weaknesses. It appears the authorities – and some staff at the hotel – have deemed him a nuisance.'

Holmes slipped the pamphlet back into his inside jacket pocket. 'The missing Henry Franke is a night manager *at* the hotel, and because his poor brother dared to bother some particularly well-placed members of society over those concerns, he is now under warning of arrest if he's found disturbing anyone further.'

'Which explains his rather audacious means of attracting our attention,' I mused.

'Exactly so!'

'But aren't the police investigating where his brother went?'

'The police,' Holmes remarked with a sigh, '*haven't* been investigating. They've not interviewed anyone. They haven't contacted a single member of the family, and so in Franke's view they've done nothing.' I could tell by the way Holmes was expressing things, the case interested him. 'Given the initial concern, I suspect the police consider it too obtuse. They may not even attempt to investigate it.'

'Obtuse in the way he disappeared?'

'Yes. As elaborate as that was, no apparent crime appears to have been committed,' Holmes said. 'I suspect the case of one missing hotel manager, known for his heavy drinking and gambling as well as several public displays of, shall we say, extramarital concerns – he'd had several affairs, so Franke said – would enjoy similar priority here as Lestrade or Bradstreet would offer in London.'

'Meaning very little.' I nodded. 'Well, if the police will do nothing, then it must fall to us,' I said firmly.

Sherlock Holmes laughed. 'Good old Watson! But to investigate such a disappearance in our country, where we would have all the advantages, would still be a significant challenge. The odds of our succeeding *here* are enormously against us.'

'It won't be easy, I agree.'

'There are *many* complications to consider first,' Holmes added. 'And if we undertake such a case, we risk coming up against the authorities.'

I nodded. 'But we have some powerful friends in this Franco organisation,' I pointed out.

'That is true. In America, power is the key to success, and knowledge is the key to gaining that power. We *might* come to rely on those connections, should the police be unhelpful,' Holmes mused. 'Our patrons *do* have financial connections everywhere, *and* long arms. But courtesy, position, even money may not be enough to persuade the police to act in our favour, especially if something or *someone* has given them a reason not to. The way they appear to have treated Henry Franke's disappearance tells us that much. How they'll even consider any requests we make, in that regard, is truly anyone's guess.' Sherlock Holmes sat in contemplative thought as he lit a second cigarette. His eyes, I observed, were relaxed and unfocused.

'Meaning we're alone?'

'I fear so, Watson,' Holmes said.

'*And* yet?' I teased.

'And... yet,' Holmes repeated, turning a grin on me. 'We will start by talking to Franke's sister-in-law. I have her address,' he said, pulling out a City of New York map. 'Are you game for a brisk walk?'

I nodded in the affirmative.

'Excellent. According to our new client, we'll find the New York equivalent of our London cab along most streets, *but* if we walk along Sixth Avenue towards Central Park, we'll find them in abundance.'

'Much like Hyde Park,' I said, chuckling. 'But why not take the streetcar?'

'Because in this instance I'd prefer we are seen using the more expensive method.'

'For appearances?'

'Indeed.'

When we'd finished our cigarettes, we crossed the street arm in arm and headed towards Sixth Avenue. When the thin grey clouds broke, revealing a bright sun, it lifted my spirits higher. I found I had a spring in my step. My body felt settled on land after being at sea for ten days, and I was enjoying the walk in the mild autumn New York air.

Sherlock Holmes directed us across another street, where he darted into the road and flagged down what could easily have been a London cab, and ushered me inside. Once Holmes had given our driver the address, we sat back in the comfortable seats, and enjoyed the ride.

Chapter Two

'The more they attempt to hide, the more I learn.'

The cab pulled up outside a very large white-marble façade apartment building that Holmes held the address for. Our fare paid, I followed Holmes as he navigated through the knee-high gardens to the correct entrance, where we were immediately met by a neatly dressed concierge who sent a similarly dressed bellhop to inform Mrs Florence Ida Franke that she had visitors. Soon after, the boy returned with an immaculately dressed, stunning-looking woman I judged to be in her early forties who extended a hand to us.

'You're Mr Holmes and Dr Watson, correct?' Mrs Franke's accent was lighter than the average, sometimes gruffer, New Yorker I'd so far met.

'We are. Thank you for agreeing to see us, madam,' my friend said, handing her his card. Her momentary look of surprise creased her otherwise smooth forehead.

'You're English?'

'Indeed,' replied Holmes. 'Your brother-in-law did not explain that?'

'No, but then I have not actually spoken with Thomas for

over a month. He sends me telegrams, sir, and that suits me well, because I cannot abide the obnoxious man.'

Mrs Franke eyed her concierge disapprovingly, whom she'd clearly caught listening to our conversation. 'Perhaps you might come in and enjoy a little privacy.'

'That would be appreciated, madam,' Holmes said.

Mrs Franke gestured to the stairs. 'If you'll follow me?'

We ascended a wide staircase to a lofty landing where Mrs Franke led us to her apartment. Once inside, a young maid – who couldn't have been any older than fifteen – took our outside apparel and Mrs Franke then invited us into a cosy sitting-room, gesturing for us to sit.

'I have coffee coming,' Mrs Franke said, 'But, if you'd prefer tea?'

'Coffee will suit us both very well,' Holmes said.

'Tommy told me you like to think out puzzles, Mr Holmes, and boy, do I have a puzzle for you?' Before Holmes could respond, Mrs Franke held up her hand at the light tap on the door, which paused our discussions. 'Ah, here's Jenny with the coffee.'

Holmes smiled as the same maid from earlier entered carrying a silver tray with a coffee pot, a set of China cups, and all the makings. She set the tray on a small table between us, and arranged the cups, but before she could continue, Mrs Franke came beside her.

'Thank you, Jenny. I'll see to my guests.' Mrs Franke's maid gave an awkward curtsey, then left.

After our hostess had poured and fixed us both coffees, my friend lifted his cup and took a sip. 'Excellent, thank you. There is nothing better than coffee to help fire the synapses. Now, in answer to your earlier question,' Holmes said, placing his cup on the table and retrieving his pipe and tobacco pouch from his jacket. 'Puzzles are my speciality. You may rely on us to investigate your concerns,' he said, lighting his now full pipe. 'But I make no promises regarding the outcome.'

'Fair,' Mrs Franke said. 'What do you need from me?'

'I should like to begin by asking you some direct questions.

Ones I hope you'll answer just as directly.'

'I have no reason not to,' our hostess said, opening a box and taking out a cigarette, which she set in a holder. Holmes lit a match, and she caught it alight. 'Ask me anything.'

'Very well. How well did you and your husband get along?'

Mrs Franke coughed as she exhaled a cloud of smoke. It was clear she wasn't a smoker. 'Starting with the tough questions, eh?' She laughed. 'Badly, Mr Holmes. Badly. We fought often. Sometimes those quarrels ended in a drunken stupor, and those were better than when they ended in violence.'

'Thank you for being so honest, Mrs Franke. And am I correct in thinking those disputes were because of Mr Franke's extramarital affairs?'

Our hostess raised an eyebrow. But if Holmes's questions had annoyed her, she did not show it. 'Investigators from England aren't like those here, that's for sure. No, *they* weren't always the result of that, but it didn't help. It might not surprise you to learn when Henry was drunk, he could be a hard man. I was perfectly happy, when he got into that state, that he found another bed to lie in.'

Holmes inclined his head. 'With your permission. I see.'

'Given…but not *gladly*. As my old dad says, to make unpleasant situations better, you're gonna need to find a compromise, if not, buy them out.'

'I understand. You are an able woman,' Holmes said.

Mrs Franke chuckled. 'Through necessity.' She eyed him through the haze of her smoke, then stubbed the cigarette out. 'I know what you're thinking.'

'Do you?' Holmes said, smoking his pipe.

'Why would I want him back?'

Holmes smiled as he nodded. 'It had crossed my mind.'

'Well, here's the thing. I have spent years with this man, moulding him, aligning his boyishness to fit my ideas of a good husband. It has taken me ten years to make him a mildly agreeable spouse, Mr Holmes, and despite all of his nonsense over the last month, I won't give up on him.'

'He began those affairs during the last month?'

Mrs Franke nodded. 'Gone for days, sometimes, but he was always here at weekends.'

My friend placed his pipe on the table and retrieved his coffee. 'Perhaps you'd detail the event of his disappearance to me?'

'Event? That's a word for it all right. We were having one of our more usual morning fights. I told Henry I'd no longer accept being the recipient of his poor behaviours, and that he could go to blazes. I heard a crash, and when I came down, his clothes were there, but he was gone. I searched. Jenny helped. But he was not in the apartment, and no one saw him leave.'

Mrs Franke sighed. 'It confounds me, still. Where did he go?'

'The doors were locked?'

'Bolted shut. Same as the windows.'

'And they'd not been opened that morning?'

'They had, because Jenny collected the morning paper. But she always bolts the door shut.'

Holmes placed his cup on the table and stood. 'Perhaps you would be kind enough to show me where you found his belongings?'

'I will, and you can also look through them, since I have them all together.'

My friend gestured for her to lead the way, and after several minutes of being shown the locations of where these events occurred – where Holmes ran his lens over everything he could – we were eventually taken to Mr Franke's bedroom, where his possessions were laid out on his neatly made bed.

'Was the bed slept in?'

'It was not.'

'And these are all the items you found when your husband disappeared?'

Mrs Franke nodded.

Holmes reviewed each article, then stood in thought for a moment. 'You say you heard the mail tray drop?'

'That's correct.'

'Where is the mail?'

Mrs Franke stared at Holmes. Her neutral expression breaking momentarily. 'There was none.'

Holmes frowned. 'You're positive there was no mail at all?'

Mrs Franke nodded, although her expression suggested she might not have been so sure.

'And who would collect any mail, Jenny?'

'Jenny, yes. The post is first sorted by Mr Swank, our nosey concierge. It's collected at six.'

I turned to Mrs Franke. 'You said before that your husband had been drinking all night?'

'As was his usual practice, Doctor, when he was given his pay.'

I raised an eyebrow in surprise. 'He spent it *all* on drink?'

Mrs Franke offered me a practiced smile. 'Not all of it, Doctor. He spends the majority on whores.' My horrified reaction provoked a kinder smile. 'It's fine. And besides, I don't need anyone's money.' At my frown, Mrs Franke said, 'I own this and everything in it.'

'The apartment?' I asked.

'The building, Doctor,' Mrs Franke replied.

I'd entered a world wholly unfamiliar. 'Forgive me, madam,' I said. 'For making assumptions.' Mrs Franke accepted my apology with grace.

Holmes then said, 'Did you hear your husband return from his night out?'

Mrs Franke turned her eyes on my friend. 'No. But I am a heavy sleeper, Mr Holmes.'

'What about Jenny?'

The question made her frown. 'I don't know.'

'Then let us ask her,' Holmes said, opening the door for Mrs Franke, who led us to a small room where Jenny was neatly folding the fresh laundry. At sight of us, the young maid attended us quickly.

'Jenny,' Mrs Franke said. 'Mr Holmes wishes to ask you some questions. Answer him honestly.'

Sherlock Holmes inclined his head to Mrs Franke, then

turned his attention to Jenny, who appeared a little intimidated by his height. 'Nothing taxing,' Holmes assured her. 'Not for such a young, diligent, and loyal woman.'

Jenny appeared embarrassed by his praise.

'You've worked for Mrs Franke for how long?'

'Five months, sir.'

'I see,' Holmes said, his nonchalant manner appearing to settle the young maid. It wouldn't be long before Holmes had her eating out of his hand.

'You enjoy working here?'

'I do. I enjoy being near the park. Or any open space,' Jenny said, adding, 'But none of that compares to the joy of serving Mrs Franke.'

Our hostess smiled at her maid.

'Jenny, you do not know me, but my name is Sherlock Holmes. I am a detective from London. We have never met, have we?'

'No, sir. Not once. I'd remember.'

Holmes nodded. 'So, I could know nothing about you.'

Jenny shrugged. 'Right. Don't see as how you could, sir?'

'I couldn't know, for example, that you like to collect sea shells—'

The maid gasped. 'Sir?'

'—but only those found near or in the ocean.'

Mrs Franke's surprise echoed my own.

'That's true, sir!' said Jenny. 'On time off, I often beachcomb for shells. How did you know?'

'When we entered, I noticed a bucket of shells by the door. They'd recently been cleaned. There was an unmistakable odour which comes only from sea-sprayed clothing. We have just spent ten days on a boat, you understand,' Holmes said with a smile. 'Now, from an observation of your hands,' he said, carefully lifting one, 'these callouses, along with those damaged nail beds, tell of long hours of domestic work. But under your nails tells a different story.'

'What do they say?' murmured Jenny.

'You've been digging,' Holmes replied. 'Digging in sand.

Those shells are yours, correct?'

The maid looked shocked. 'Yes, sir.'

'And you collected them this morning?'

Jenny nodded. 'You're a wizard!'

'I'm simply observant. There's a certain spirituality in your face that tells of time free of other concerns.' My friend then let go of her hand. 'I hope that small demonstration helps you to recognise, I see far more than people might choose to tell me. The more they attempt to hide, the more I learn. So then, isn't it just better to be frank?'

Jenny simply nodded.

'Then let's review the day your master disappeared, shall we? Can you tell me what you remember?'

'Certainly, sir. Mr Franke came from his room and collected his morning paper. I saw him in the foyer and then went to my kitchen duties. I heard a crash and arrived at the same times as Mrs Franke to find Mr Franke gone.'

'And he was alone at the moment of his disappearance?'

'He was.'

'And what were you doing at the time?'

'Filling the laundry basket, sir.'

My friend then said, 'And what did you do with the letter he received?'

Mrs Franke appeared surprised. 'There was no letter,' she said.

Holmes turned to Jenny. 'Is that so?'

'Yes,' she replied.

Holmes held up a finger. 'No, no. We agreed to be frank, did we not?'

She looked shocked. 'Well, yes, sir.'

'There was mail that morning,' Holmes calmly restated.

'No, sir!'

'If you do not wish to feel the *full* weight of the law raining down upon you,' Holmes said, his friendly demeanour gone, 'you will tell me what you did with that letter.'

'Oh, sir,' the young maid wailed. 'I don't know *what* you mean.'

Mrs Franke turned to Holmes. 'If Jenny says there's no letter, then there's *no* letter. Bullying the girl half to death won't get you anything!'

'Your husband was holding a mail tray, Mrs Franke. Why would he do so, unless he was collecting the mail?' It was obvious by Mrs Franke's expression that Holmes had intrigued her. Perhaps that's why she did not object to his continuing to question her maid further. Holmes slipped his hand into his left pocket and retrieved a torn edge of a scrap of blue paper. 'Do you recognise this?'

Jenny's mouth opened wide. Her eyes filled with tears. She looked between Holmes and Mrs Franke, the colour leaving her face. 'I swear I never saw what was in it!'

Holmes nodded. 'You left a letter on the tray for Mr Franke. A letter written on expensive blue stationery. One you'd collected earlier with the newspaper, correct?'

Tears fell down her cheeks, but she still said nothing.

'It will be a straightforward thing to corroborate it with Mr Swank,' Holmes said. Jenny's tears flowed faster as she nodded. 'It appears as though this letter was pulled out of his hand, but he kept the tiny fragment he'd ripped off. I found it in his possessions. During that scuffle, it is my belief that he dropped the tray. Soon after, he vanished.' Holmes leant towards her. 'Since people don't spontaneously disappear, there must be another answer, and I believe it lies with you. You're a proven liar, Jenny – if that's even your real name. Now, I'll ask you again. *What* did you do with that letter?'

'He took it,' Jenny muttered.

'Did he? Was that before you assisted his escape through the laundry basket?'

The maid nodded. I glanced at Mrs Franke, who had fixed her eyes on Jenny. 'What?'

Homes turned to her. 'There was only one way your husband could conceivably have left the apartment, madam, and that was with help. To leave entirely unobserved is impossible, so I theorised he was either still here, or had a means by which he could leave. And once here, I deduced the laundry basket provided those means. No one is likely to look inside until they empty it.' Holmes returned to the maid. 'All that remains for you to do now is explain why.'

Jenny shook her head. 'I'm *not* to tell!' she cried.

Mrs Franke pushed passed Holmes in order, I thought, to comfort the girl. I could not have been more wrong. Mrs Frank grabbed Jenny's arm, roughly pulling her onto her feet. She then marched the trembling girl into the sitting-room, where she deposited her onto a settee, and calmly said, 'You'd better tell.' Mrs Franke's expression turned outwardly dangerous. 'Or so help me, I'll make sure you, your friend, your entire family never find work in this or any other city, ever again.'

Mrs Franke's shocking threat did its work, as Jenny blurted her entire story through incoherent wailing. The crux of which was, Mrs Franke's husband had paid her maid to assist in his… escape. To say it annoyed Mrs Franke would be to underestimate her level of anger. She was furious. She dismissed her maid there and then, sending her away with a stark warning that the promise she'd made earlier stood.

Holmes and I remained as dispassionate as we could – he perhaps having less of a time with that aspect than I – while Mrs Franke straightened herself out. Calmly, she said, 'Find him, Mr Holmes. If you do, I'll give you anything you want.'

My friend smiled. 'There is only one thing I would ask for,' he said.

'Name it.'

'A pardon for that young woman. She wasn't to blame. *You* put her in that terrible position. You and your husband.'

It was clear Mrs Franke was unused to being spoken to so sternly. She slowly stood to meet his gaze, her eyes of steel, then they softened and she inclined her head. 'Agreed.'

Holmes nodded. 'Come, Watson,' he said, leaving me to give our goodbyes.

* * *

'That was decidedly unpleasant,' I said, as I followed Holmes toward a coffee shop at the corner of Central Park. New Yorkers, it seemed, were hardy people. Many of the patrons were seated outside despite the cool air. 'Who is Mrs Franke, really?'

'The daughter of Henry Royce Greene, an industrialist and philanthropist. He helped lead the expansion of the American coal industry, and it made him a very wealthy man.'

'How do you know that?'

Holmes opened the door to the café, waited for me to enter, then following behind. 'He's one of the richest men in New York, Watson, and Mrs Franke is his heir,' Holmes said as we took a table.

'Is she an only child?'

Holmes took out a travel *Who's Who* and flicked through the pages. 'No, there are three children. Girls. She is the oldest, and since he has no male heir, she will inherit the larger share of his almost four-hundred-million-dollar fortune.'

'We've entered a fairy-tale land,' I said, sitting back in my chair. 'It seems Henry Franke would end up being a wealthy man, so why would he have a maid assist his leaving, in such a convoluted way?'

'Well, because some people are superstitious, Watson. They believe in tales of spontaneous disappearances. These people are also some of the wealthiest in the country, most probably the world. Real world concerns, such as these, hardly matter to them at all. Mrs Franke wants her husband returned because to her he is property.'

'That's immoral, Holmes.'

'I know,' my friend soothed.

We paused our conversation when a young server put a pot and cups onto the table. 'I hope you don't mind, but when I heard them English voices, I just went and made a pot of English tea.'

'Very thoughtful,' Holmes said. The girl offered him a smile, then she went to another table.

'So what are we going to do about Henry Franke?' I asked,

savouring the powerful brew.

'Find him, of course.'

I frowned. 'But perhaps he doesn't want to go back?'

Holmes took out his pipe and cleaned it. 'I said I'd find him, Watson. So that is what I shall do. We also have a young woman's future in our hands. Sadly, if we wish to help Jenny, we must act as we've agreed to do.'

I nodded. 'It might go badly for us if we don't. She seems a pretty vindictive woman.'

'She just rich, Watson. They think differently from the rest of us.'

That was certainly true. 'So, where do we go next?'

'We wait,' Holmes said, stuffing a pipe.

I sipped my coffee for a while in silence, turning my eye to the windows, admiring the opulent landscape as Holmes furiously smoked beside me.

* * *

'There,' Holmes said, standing. 'Quickly, Watson.' He dropped coins on our table and darted away, with me attempting to catch up, whilst struggling to get into my jacket. Fortunately, he'd stopped by a tree, making it possible for me to come alongside.

'What—'

Holmes shushed me, indicating I should get in close behind, while he peeked ahead. Eventually, I poked my head around him and saw the object of his excitement. It was Jenny, and she was talking to one of the young bellhops from the apartment. When he left, she lowered her head and shuffled away. Holmes gestured for us to follow.

Jenny turned off Fifth Avenue at Sixty-Third Street and we followed, keeping our distance.

'I think she's heading for the estuary,' Holmes said, pulling me behind a merchant's wagon. He eyed the road and surrounding buildings. I could tell he was on alert. He narrowed his eyes. 'I don't like the feel of this, Watson.'

'What's wrong?'

Just then a Brougham with three black horses, each with an ostrich-feathered bridle, turned sharply into the street. The sound of it made us turn. Then, from places around us, we heard a strange call of "why-oh" being chanted by several people, from different locations. Holmes looked around us and growled. His eyes turned to the carriage and when he stepped into the road, he immediately put a hand to his face and stepped backwards, colliding with me.

'They're using mirrors to blind us,' I cried.

'Get back, Watson!' Holmes yelled.

I felt my arm being pulled as I stumbled back, narrowly avoiding the carriage that came at speed between us and Jenny, and when it passed, she was gone.

'Where did she go?' I asked, stepping into the road, but Holmes stopped me.

'Come, Watson,' my friend said, urgently steering me away. His expression suggested now was not the time to discuss it. We walked at a brisk pace, Holmes matching mine since my wound could sometimes affect my speed. 'Keep your eyes forward,' Holmes murmured.

This wasn't the first time I'd been in a sticky situation, both with and without Holmes. I was an ex-soldier, so I'd had my share of dangers. But, aside from David Wilkinson – who was pretty solid in a pinch – there wasn't another person alive I'd rather be with in a dangerous situation than Sherlock Holmes.

'From where?'

'Everywhere.' Holmes directed me under a barber's awning and then we turned onto Third Avenue. Holmes remained on high alert. I did not know if these threats to us were real or perceived, but either way I was glad when he directed us towards a two-horse streetcar. We got aboard and I was about to sit when Holmes pointed to the road, and jumped off. I quickly followed, before the car built up speed, and caught up with Holmes, who'd somehow hailed a passing cab. Once we were aboard, he pointed to the streetcar. 'Look.'

I observed three rough-looking men jump out, and they

were all looking in our direction.

'What just happened?' I asked, but I could not draw Holmes on any topic of conversation, so I settled in my seat and ran through the events as we headed back to our hotel.

Chapter Three

'We may have the will, but not the city's knowledge or labour force.'

Sherlock Holmes said nothing until we'd left the carriage and entered our suite of rooms. As soon as we were alone, he immediately began uttering a series of unprintable profanities. Holmes was not an emotional man, and it was therefore unusual for me to hear him express his frustrations this way. I have learnt, painfully, that one must wait until he is ready to speak before engaging him, especially when he was in this type of mood. It wasn't a surprise to me when he curled himself up in his chair, closed his eyes, and began puffing away on his clay pipe – the one, incidentally, he often choses when his mood turns sour.

Not wanting to be the recipient of any ill feeling or agitation, I crept into the second of our three rooms and poured a fresh coffee from the pot a bellhop had just delivered. I took it to the window, where for an hour I sat and drank coffee and smoked a cigar – all the time enjoying the wonderful view of the stunning Madison Square Park, formed by the intersection of Fifth Avenue and Broadway.

'It simply won't do!' Holmes growled, as he threw open the interconnecting door, startling me awake me from my nap. I yawned and stretched, and evaluated my friend's mood as he collected a coffee from the table. His outburst had sounded severe, but his expression was unreadable. When he joined me at the chairs I'd positioned earlier at the large window, he fell into his with a great sigh.

'It would help if you explained,' I cautiously said, stifling another yawn.

Holmes looked at me as if for the first time. 'Oh, my dear fellow, I'm sorry to have woken you.'

'No, think nothing of it. I knew to give you time to think things through.'

'You are a saint, Watson,' my friend said. 'I have made a grievous error, and at this moment, am unsure how to rectify it.'

'This is to do with the girl, Jenny?'

My friend nodded. 'I foolishly accepted Mrs Franke at her word.'

I frowned. 'Meaning what?'

Holmes sighed. 'I may be directly responsible for that girl's death, Watson.'

'Surely not? Why would anyone want to kill her?'

'Because she dared to defy a wealthy benefactor, and now is probably paying the consequences. Imbecile!'

I now understood his earlier outburst. 'You think Mrs Franke will enact her threats, despite her agreement with you?'

Holmes sipped his coffee. 'I think her capable of *far* worse. The question that beats against my skull is this: Was she taken, or did she flee? That carriage blocked our view for approximately twenty-six-seconds, and in that time, Jenny had vanished. Each scenario I come up with suggests the former. Which puts her – and by definition us – in significant danger.'

'Perhaps we should call the police?'

Holmes shook his head. 'Not until we know a little more. When the situation warrants it, I have a contact I can call. Until then we must determine things for ourselves. You saw those rough fellows we narrowly escaped from at the streetcar?'

'Indeed, they looked a little like lumberyard workers.'

'Labourers certainly. Given their coveralls, I am more inclined to suggest a metal works.'

I shrugged. 'As you say.'

'But who sent them, Watson? Was it Mr or Mrs Franke?'

I nodded.

Holmes smiled at me. 'You understand the dilemma we now face? Both husband *and* wife have an interest in that girl's silence.'

'And if Mrs Franke has reneged on her agreement, that frees you.'

Holmes shook his head. 'Sadly, it's not that simple. There is no proof Mrs Franke has taken any action against our agreement, and should I call her out for her sly boldness, I'll make *us* a target. Mrs Franke's family are part of the elite in this vast city, but although her position in the social order may not rank higher than those who would go to bat for us at the Franco-American Union, her father is an entirely different proposition.'

'And if it *was* Mr Franke?'

'Then either he wishes to buy her silence, or else…'

'I see. Then it is imperative we find this girl then!'

Holmes looked out at the park. '*If* she's still alive. And even if she were, the task you suggest would be impossible. We are out of our depth here, Watson.' He sat back in his chair. 'We may have the will, but *not* the city's knowledge or labour force.'

I smiled at him. 'We don't *need* either, Holmes. We have something better, and it's right here in the hotel.'

Holmes frowned momentarily, then his expression brightened, and he laughed. '*What* has happened to the brains God has given me? The porter network!'

'The porter network,' I echoed.

Sherlock Holmes turned his smile towards the window. 'Yes,' he said. 'I think that might work.'

Although it wasn't that late, the sun was setting and it had been quite a first introduction to America.

'Let us have dinner, then retire for the evening,' Holmes said. 'It has been a long day, and we're likely to have a longer one tomorrow.'

After we'd eaten, I returned to my seat by the window and looked out at the gardens below, which looked entirely different in the darkness. Eventually, I took myself to bed.

* * *

The following morning, after our breakfast, Holmes introduced us to a young porter named Daniel Wiseman, an average-height, lanky, dark-haired man of twenty-five. A keen musician *and* amateur boxer, Wiseman was two years married with a baby on the way. He'd worked various positions at several of the large hotels in the city since he was thirteen, and currently held a senior porter position at this hotel, one he'd held for the past three years. He was certainly qualified for the job we were about to ask him to do.

My friend laid out the situation in great detail, and the young Wiseman listened carefully. We actually had no trouble convincing him to help, since Henry Franke had been his manager and mentor, and they were close. There was a lengthy discussion regarding money, which they finally agreed on, and the interview ended with Wiseman and Holmes shaking hands.

My friend gave our new ally a comprehensive description of Jenny – whose last name we were never told – and the address of Mrs Franke's apartment, how she was in the situation she was in, and where she'd disappeared.

'The carriage that passed us was a Brougham. Black wooden panels, with a silver floral motif of a rose, its petals rolled at the top, centred on each door. A fully enclosed carriage, with dark curtained windows—'

'And three black horses, each with a white ostrich-feathered plume on their bridle?'

Holmes raised an eyebrow. 'Indeed. You've seen this carriage before?'

'I'm looking at it right now, sir,' Wiseman said, pointing to the window.

We turned and observed that carriage sitting on the road next to Madison Square Park. Wiseman tipped his hat.

'If you gents will excuse me?' the young porter said, and left.

I turned to Holmes, who was looking through the telescopic lens on one of his canes. 'Can you make anything out?'

Holmes nodded. 'The occupant.'

'Is it Mrs Franke?'

'No,' Holmes said, turning an odd expression my way. He stood and crossed the room, returning with a flyer I'd seen earlier on a billboard. 'Maximillian's Park of Amusements,' Holmes said, handing me his scope and the flyer. 'And if I'm not mistaken, that's Maximillian sitting in that carriage.'

I looked through the telescopic lens and compared the fellow in the carriage to the face printed on the flyer. 'That's him.'

A porter walked over to the cab and I handed the scope back to Holmes. I observed the young fellow speaking with the occupant, who waved his arm as the porter jumped back in time for the carriage to lurch away. Just then another smaller porter leapt out from behind a shrubbery and landed on the carriage's luggage rack, and rode it away.

'These young fellows are *dazzlingly* bright,' Holmes said, then disappeared out of the room.

Several hours later, I checked my pocket watch for what felt like the hundredth time. It was fast approaching time for dinner and as Holmes had not returned, I left a note explaining my intention to head to the dining-room. The likelihood Holmes would eat, if he did show, was small anyway, so I didn't feel too guilty. As my menu had already been chosen – one of many first-class perks – I simply had to arrive and a table would be waiting.

I had just poured a second glass from a fine bottle of Château

Mouton Rothschild, which had been paired beautifully with the beef bourguignon that had just been placed before me, when I was happy to see Holmes. He took the empty chair opposite, and was immediately attended to by the maître d'hôtel, who made several recommendations – all excellent – which I expected him to reject. But my friend surprised me by not doing so. Medical science did not back his habit of refusing to eat so, as he described, the energy could be reserved exclusively for his brain, with none being wasted on digestion. Holmes, being ever vigilant, smiled at me as he removed his cigarette case from his pocket, placing it and his matches onto the table. My friend demonstrated frequently how he could easily read me and my thoughts, so when he lit a cigarette and said, 'When in Rome,' I simply chuckled.

'What did you learn from Wiseman?'

'Some useful data about the workings of the city, but nothing regarding the case. These fellows are very smart. Did you see how they distracted the occupant and driver whilst a second snuck aboard unseen? They have brains, especially Wiseman. He is a first-class boxer, Watson. He's a little scrappy, and his footwork requires serious attention, but he's intuitive and capable of adapting – and quickly. During a friendly spar, he improved swiftly. It was enough to elevate him into a more challenging opponent. And his prose, Watson, is remarkable. He has written a book of sonnets which he hopes to publish soon.'

While I waited for my beef to cool, I nibbled on the bread. A server added a bottle of Californian white wine to the table, and it was shortly followed by Holmes's halibut in hollandaise sauce. The wait and kitchen staff's expeditiousness meant Holmes and I could eat together.

Our meal lasted around thirty minutes, and we talked on and off about the differences between the American and British cultures. We certainly appeared to intrigue our Atlantic cousins, who appeared ready to engage us in conversation, at any moment, often in inappropriate places, and unaware of their recipient's level of interest – which for American politics, in my case, was non-existent. The cultural differences we share and pay little attention to, until face-to-face, interested me more. Typically, British people are more reserved and, dare I say it, politer than our American counterparts. We British have a strong sense of tradition, with an emphasis on our history and heritage, and in contrast, Americans appeared more open-minded and outspoken, especially in expressing opinions or beliefs. I found those interactions to be a bit of a mixed bag, for my level interests.

I enjoyed meeting medical colleagues, including an ostentatiously loud dentist, who claimed to have taken care of some big names, and a pharmacist who erroneously claimed several standard remedies as his own concoctions – and would not budge from his "truth" since he had never left America, and did not ever plan to. I failed to catch *his* name, because a young fellow carrying an armful of books dropped a stack onto our table and then begged Holmes to sign them, who obliged him, since they were a collection of monographs on various topics he'd written over the years, stamped "Masonic Hall library, 23rd and Sixth." When the collection of people had left us, Holmes gestured to the maître d'hôtel and asked if he could dissuade any further visitors.

Once we'd consumed a strong coffee, and a slice of peach shortcake neither of us had tried before – it was excellent incidentally – we ended our second night's dining experience by taking brandy in our exclusive smoking lounge, where I collected a cigar and sat opposite my friend who had stuffed and lit his pipe. Settled, I was enjoying our contemplative after-meal quiet, when a heavy red-faced fellow with a huge black moustache and slicked-back thinning speckled black-grey hair interrupted our meditations with a question.

'Which one of you fellas is Holmes?' The man looked between us as he traded the cigar he was smoking for an obnoxiously large brandy, from which he took a huge slurp – some of its contents apparently missing his rather sizable mouth.

'Who is asking?' Holmes said. I remained silent.

The fellow coughed on his cigar and just stared down at us. It was difficult to say if he was annoyed or amused, possibly both. Given where we were, and how much these fellows liked to brag about their wealth, I suspect he was unused to not being recognised. The portly fellow leant back and belly-laughed – for an awkwardly long time – then to Holmes he said, 'You're Holmes. There's an arrogance about you. A smugness, just behind the eyes…and sitting in an opulence you clearly dislike—'

'Indeed,' Holmes said, raising an eyebrow, but the fellow wasn't ready to be interrupted.

'—yet tolerate. I know you, sir. Like I know myself. Success brought you here, and you reek of it. I've seen it. Frequently. Every time I look in a mirror.' There was a brief pause as Holmes stood, a smile on his lips. The fellow also smiled, then extended his hand.

'It is a pleasure to meet you, Mr Henry Royce Greene,' Holmes said. The fact Holmes appeared to recognise the American magnate pleased him. Hearing the name caused me to cough on *my* cigar. I instantly stood and extended my hand, which he took.

'My friend and colleague, Doctor Watson,' Holmes said. 'Won't you sit?'

Greene undid a button on his vast waistcoat and sat in the chair beside us. Mrs Franke's vastly wealthy father gulped another mouthful from his glass.

'To what do we owe the pleasure?' Holmes said, catching his pipe with a match.

Greene swilled his brandy, then swallowed, lifting his bowl again – the ridiculous thing had to be three times the size of ours – and stared at Holmes over the rim. There appeared to be a contest of wills between them, but it ended when Mr Greene broke eye contact and took a moderate sip.

'You found that foolish son-in-law of mine yet?'

Holmes removed his pipe from his mouth. 'I have only just taken the case. Yesterday, in fact.'

Greene narrowed his eyes. 'That's not a *no*, Mr Holmes.'

'It isn't,' Holmes agreed.

'They say you're the greatest detective in the world.'

Holmes laughed. '*They* exaggerate.'

'Let's cut to the chase then. I earn more in a minute than some people earn in a year. I'm not one to bandy words or waste time. Have you found him or not?'

Holmes considered him for a moment. 'I have not.'

'I see. But would you tell me if you had?' Greene asked.

'Since you don't wish to waste time or words, here's my answer. No, I would not. Mr Franke's brother is my client, Mr Greene. Not you.'

If Greene had been annoyed by Holmes's directness, he did not display it. 'And if I made it my business to know?'

Holmes offered him a fleeting smile. 'This is *your* city, Mr Greene, not mine. You have significant control of it and I could not stop you from doing so.'

'Well said. And if I should also attempt to make it worth your while to come over to my side, what would you say to that?'

The idea was undignified, and I knew Holmes well enough to say it would certainly dissuade him, but this was a high-level game between two experienced players. I kept my thoughts to myself.

Holmes appeared more amused than annoyed by Greene's suggestion. 'I should warn you, sir. I'm entirely unlike any previous *lackey* you might have bought and paid for.'

Henry Royce Greene roared with laughter. It appeared to settle him. 'An incorruptible man in a city built on exploitation? That'll make for an interesting show. I appreciate frankness, Mr Holmes. People call it rude. I call it *timesaving*. Since I now know I cannot persuade you to say anything on the matter, might you at least *listen* to a father's perspective?'

Holmes inclined his head. 'It would be my pleasure to do so, Mr Greene.'

'Then here it is: I'd prefer it if we never saw Henry Franke again.'

'I see. That appears a rather callous statement, since we do not yet know if Mr Franke has come to any actual harm.'

'And we certainly wouldn't wish for *that*,' Greene said, firmly. 'But for my daughter's future, I'd be willing to ignore her wishes, and pay you to see that he never returns. However you feel it needs doing is fine, but leave me out of the details.'

Holmes smiled. 'I suspected that to be your position, Mr Greene. I recognise how valuable your time is, so to make that case in person is sincerely appreciated, but there are several complications that cannot be ignored.'

'Such as?'

'Aside from the morally objectionable suggestion, I am already engaged, sir.'

'By Franke's brother, yes. The two requests appear to have a mutual concern, do they not? You find Franke, you fulfil your client's request – all is well – and if you persuade him to leave, you'll fulfil mine, and I'll make you rich. It's a win for both. Where's the harm?'

'It is not my usual practice to take on another client for the same case, but we are in foreign territory. I do believe there may be benefits for us both, but I would have conditions.'

'Of course,' Greene said, nodding.

'I also do not believe I'm breaking any confidences by saying we have another concern regarding your daughter's maid. In fact, it is *chief* amongst them.'

Greene frowned. 'Jenny? Well, I'm sure it must *seem* difficult, Mr Holmes, especially to someone who hasn't engaged many domestics, but let me assure you, sir, it *really* isn't. We can *easily* find her another maid.'

Holmes frowned. 'I fear you have missed the point, Mr Greene. Jenny has disappeared under what you might call mysterious circumstances.'

'I did not know that,' Greene said, and appeared genuinely concerned. 'I certainly do not wish that young girl any complications, but she did bring this on her own head.'

'True,' Holmes said. 'And as I ousted her, I do bear some responsibility for what happens next. And in that regards, I do urge you to have a second discussion with your daughter.'

Mr Greene's eyes narrowed. 'You're suggesting my girl has some involvement in that?'

'I suggest nothing,' Holmes replied politely. 'Your daughter made severe overtures regarding it, but as I do not know if she would action them, I turn to you, Mr Greene, because you know her better.'

'When my daughter has decided, I *might* struggle to change her from it. You say she has made open threats to her maid?'

Holmes nodded. 'To her maid and anyone she might know, apparently. This happened as Jenny was dismissed.'

'For *betraying* her mistress's interests, Holmes. Even though I might say she was right to, for personal reasons, she was still a paid employee. When such a grievous betrayal occurs, I challenge anyone not to remove them.'

'I am not attempting to pass comment on Mrs Franke's actions as an employer. That is no business of mine. I simply *recommend* you have as frank a discussion with her as you are having with me, since I have given you additional information that might change an opinion? That is all.'

'I see. You've clearly never had children, Holmes.'

'You are correct. Are things so different here then, that a daughter might ignore the advice of her father, *Mr* Greene?'

The heavyset man chuckled. 'Touché, *Mr* Holmes.' Greene grunted as he stood, and we followed him. 'I understand what you're asking. Very well. I like you,' Greene said, handing him a business card. 'You and your companion will come for dinner. The day after tomorrow. Gives us an opportunity for things to get straightened out, if you follow?'

It didn't appear to be an optional dinner, I thought.

'I do,' Holmes answered. 'And we'd be delighted to accept your generous invitation, Mr Greene,' Holmes said on behalf of us both. I knew there was no way Holmes could have declined.

'Thank you, sir,' I said.

Greene turned to me. 'I understand you're an Army surgeon?'

I nodded. 'Civilian practise now, though. My first posting

was—'

'Good for you, Doctor!' Greene turned to Holmes. 'Two days from now,' he said, pointing at him. 'Cocktails at six o'clock sharp. I cannot abide unpunctuality, sirs, so arrive fifteen minutes early.' The American magnate chomped down on his cigar, and took his massive empty brandy glass out with him.

Sherlock Holmes's eyes remained fixed on the door, long after it had closed.

'What an interesting man,' I mused.

'Yes, but what did he *really* want, eh?'

'As brash and unconnected to reality as most of these wealthy people are, I thought his motives were pretty clear.'

'He presents us with a serious dilemma, this Mr Greene. The fact he should know or display any concern for his daughter's domestic speaks volumes. He knew her *name*, Watson, and seemed genuinely troubled when we referred to her odd disappearance. He's an astute man. Observant, analytical. I do not think his daughter makes a habit of routinely lying to him. It suggests she's innocent of Jenny's abduction.'

'But we can't know that for certain,' I said.

'No, we cannot. But the probability lies in that direction, especially if you interpret all the information gathered to date contextually. So, if Jenny *was* abducted, was it out of concern for her well-being, or is she in mortal danger?'

Those were two pretty different reasons. 'I see, and you think we might consider it was for her well-being?'

Holmes shrugged. 'I do not know that with any real certainty.'

'We have two days to discover some answers then,' I said.

'Which must happen tomorrow,' Holmes said, standing.

'You off to bed?' It was still early, but Holmes could keep very odd hours when engaged.

'No, I have several enquires to make tonight,' my friend said.

'Should I make ready to join you?' I dutifully asked.

'Not tonight,' Holmes said, smiling. 'Rest. Where I must go requires not only a guide, but a change of appearance as well.'

'Ah, you intend to go undercover somewhere with Wiseman?'

Holmes nodded. 'Learn the lay of the land,' he said. 'And if it's a useful exercise, I'll explain more in the morning.'

'Then I wish you happy hunting,' I said.

'Good night, Watson,' Holmes said, and he too then left the room.

Chapter Four

'The fellow dresses in a tuxedo the entire day and smokes profusely.'

Saturday morning was bright and brisk, cooler by degrees than the previous day. I therefore chose my larger overcoat for my walk. It was remarkable how different an autumn in New York felt to London. This was mostly because, unlike in England, here there was no lack of sunshine. It cheered me up, and it apparently kept most of the New Yorkers I'd met cheerful too. I regarded a blue cloudless sky and smiled. It had taken a while for my body to get used to the differences in time, and by now my sleeping pattern had normalised. Ahead, along the *relatively* clean pavement, I spotted my objective. A newspaper seller. I picked up copies of the *New York Herald* and *Times*, then headed a little further along Fifth Avenue, taking in the sights. Both those newspapers were available at the hotel – like anything else I might want for – but the desire to collect my own was born from a routine exercise I maintained daily, to ensure my old wound was kept in check, and also because I always thought better when ambulating.

When I returned to the hotel, I took breakfast and then

coffee in the adjoining smoking room. It was there I found Holmes, reading a copy of the *London Times*, albeit a few days old.

'There you are, Watson,' Holmes said, dropping his newspaper. 'Did you sleep well?'

'I did. Did you?'

Holmes folded his paper and smiled. 'I caught a few winks.'

'And how did you do last night?'

'It was quite an experience. Wiseman took me to several clubs and places of interest. With his help, I established myself as a visiting veterinarian from Detroit.'

'Veterinary medicine seems a tough profession to mimic. Why choose that occupation?'

'Well, in this city there are somewhere near, perhaps, four thousand of them.'

I was astounded. 'Really? Is there such a high demand then?'

Holmes nodded. 'This city, like London, is horse powered, Watson. Of course there's a high demand. Relatively few individual city dwellers own a horse because the animals are expensive to keep. That's why people rely on cabs, or omnibuses and streetcars.' Holmes removed his pipe from his jacket and filled it. 'Last year in London there were over eleven thousand hansom cabs on the streets alone. Adding to that several thousand horse-drawn buses, each needing twelve horses per day, made a staggering total of over fifty thousand horses transporting people around the city each day.'

'I did not know the numbers were that high, but I know that the manure problem gets progressively worse because of it.'

'Indeed, but *this* city, Watson, eclipses that by degrees. According to a *Herald* article, the New York Department of Street Cleaning removed fifteen thousand dead horses from the streets last year—'

'Good lord!'

'—with one analyst suggesting a city horse would fall on average every ninety-six miles it travelled. There were approximately one hundred and thirty thousand horses depositing around a million pounds of manure, each day.'

'I see now why you'd choose that profession.'

Holmes lit his pipe and blew out the match. 'I can go anywhere there is a horse, almost with impunity. Hardly anyone will question why.'

'Unless they have a genuine emergency,' I pointed out.

Holmes did not respond to that.

'Why Detroit?'

My friend smiled at me. 'No one I've spoken to has ever been there, or knows anyone who lives there. It was a perfect choice because any mistakes in accent, colloquialisms, or slang might easily be overlooked since Detroit is about as foreign a place as England is.'

'Then why not just be English?' I wondered aloud.

'Well, despite their open-mindedness, Americans are far more welcoming of their own and are likely to be less guarded because of it.'

That made sense. 'So, you've successfully created this persona to gather information?'

Holmes nodded. 'Amongst other things. Now, are you ready for an adventure?' The smile he gave caused me to chuckle.

'Of course.'

'Then gather what you need for the next two days, since it's likely we're to return the following day.'

'Where are we going?' I asked. Holmes handed me the Maximillian's Park of Amusements flyer. 'Ah, you've discovered his location, then?'

'Wiseman's boy reported back with the address last night. He's staying at the Bull's Head on Third Avenue, Twenty-Fourth Street.'

'You intend to go there first?'

Holmes shook his head. 'I intend to take the Communipaw Ferry to the Central Railroad of New Jersey Terminal—'

'From there, we'll travel to this park?' I interrupted.

'Yes. We must return the following day if we are to keep

our appointment with Mr Greene.'

'And in the meantime, you hope to discover something new regarding Jenny's location?'

'Bravo, Watson. You're positively sizzling.'

I laughed. 'But, is it possible this Maximillian has nothing at all to do with the case?'

Holmes gave me a look. 'You think I'd make us travel to this park in a neighbouring state on a whim?'

'No,' I admitted. 'Clearly you know more than I do.'

'Perhaps just a little more,' Holmes said with a wink. His mood was infectious.

'Then I shall get myself together. Will twenty minutes work?'

'Perfectly,' Holmes said, checking a railway timetable. 'That gives us more than enough time to get the Newark train at the terminal.'

* * *

Sherlock Holmes was waiting inside the Fifth Avenue Transportation Company cab when I stepped onto the hotel concourse. One of many things I liked about New York was its roads. They were laid in straight lines vertically and horizontally. It meant we could stay on Broadway for our entire journey.

'How long before we get to the ferry?'

Holmes had his map spread across his knees. 'The journey is approximately two and a half miles, so I estimate we'll arrive at the foot of Liberty Street in around thirty to forty minutes.'

'Quicker than expected,' I said.

After we'd paid our cab fare, Holmes directed us to the Communipaw Ferry office, where we purchased out tickets, and soon after we boarded at pier fourteen. When the last person was accommodated, the gate was closed and the steamer took us the short ride to the Central Railroad of New Jersey Terminal.

Around an hour later we boarded into our comfortable first-class cabin, and settled in. The journey to Newark was roughly a two-hour ride. Once we arrived Holmes was confident that we'd find a carriage and driver to take us to the park.

'What do you know of this Maximillian? Anything?'

'His full name is Cornelius Mathias Maximillian,' Holmes said, in between long pulls of his pipe. 'Born in Brooklyn, in 1864, Maximillian's family worked and lived on Coney Island. He followed in his father's footsteps and became an engineer. A young Maximillian assisted in the installation of the first Switchback Railway rollercoaster there. And would later take those designs and build his own version with help from several wealthy benefactors – one of which, I have discovered, is our friend Mr Greene.'

'What an amazingly small world,' I remarked.

Holmes chuckled. 'Shockingly so. It *is* as solid a connection as one could wish for, without doubt.'

'So, how does this switch railway work?'

'It is gravity based, Watson. Riders sit upon benches in a carriage atop a tower, from which they coast at speed down a straight track, undulating up and down, to a second tower. Upon reaching that tower, the carriage is switched to a second track which carries them back.'

'Ah, hence *Switchback*,' I said.

'But both Coney Island and Maximillian's rides were later replaced by a complete-circuit track, traversing an oval rather than a straight track. Maximillian calls his The Punisher.'

I shook my head in wonder. 'I did not know you had *any* interest, nor also that these fancies were becoming more prevalent.'

'To call them fancies, Watson, is to deny the very real scientific advancements and value they represent. With each new idea comes an exploration of physics in its plainest form. We know about the natural forces, but these fellows get to experience those forces and contextualise them. The data gathered might one day teach us how to harness those very forces, and perhaps because of that, who knows? Horseless carriages are not a fantasy. And should they become more commonplace and save tens of thousands of horses a year as a result, then I'm all for it. It is an *incredibly* exciting time scientifically.'

Sherlock Holmes had a voracious appetite for scientific advances, and I admit the idea we might save those horses' lives felt as though it would be worth it. And not having to breathe the foul stench of manure as a result was something, I suspect, we'd *all* be happier with. 'I retract my statement then, and say bravo to the innovators. But didn't this fellow Maximillian simply take another person's idea and recreate it for his own profit?'

'I believe they call it the New American Dream, oh, and capitalism.'

'And you know all of this because?'

'I talked with Maximillian last night,' Holmes replied. 'An interesting character, whose arrogant self-proclamations make him a decidedly unlikeable fellow.'

'He sounds nice,' I said, laughing.

My friend mirrored my amusement. 'Oh, he's delightful. You'll get to meet him soon to see for yourself. He dresses in a tuxedo the entire day and smokes profusely.' Holmes smiled at me. 'The fellow has fattened on his good living and become morally reprehensible through money. Honestly, Watson. His repugnance makes our more deranged nobility seem slightly more civilized.'

I laughed. 'I'm looking forward to our meeting,' I said.

'Originally an entrepreneur, he now has interests around the city that extend to New Jersey. One of his largest backers being the aforementioned Henry Royce Green. I gained what information I could but it wasn't much.'

'Since Mr Greene is an investor do you think this Maximillian is bought and paid for too?'

'I don't think so, Watson, but I cannot say for certain My observations suggest the fellow wouldn't allow *anyone* a claw in him for anything. He is successfully and independently wealthy, although not in same category as Greene, nevertheless comfortable.'

'These rich fellows hold no loyalty to people like us, Holmes. Do you think Jenny is at his park?'

Holmes remained thoughtful. 'I am working on two theories that both link to Maximillian. I believe Jenny *is* there, but what condition we find her in I cannot predict.'

For most of that journey, we sat in quiet contemplation, where I reflected on the bizarre circumstances that had led us here. I recalled details of conversations, using the quiet to update my notes. And then my mind wandered. I considered the route we'd taken, but what I struggled to quantify was *what* we were investigating.

Our first case of a missing person in a city of around two and a half million would never be a straightforward thing to investigate, let alone find a solution for. Holmes pointed out that people in cities often disappear. The trick was to determine whether they were forced or coerced to leave unwillingly. If the newspapers are to be believed, nameless bodies wash up along most of the rivers almost daily.

But against all the odds, Holmes had *somewhat* solved Henry Franke's disappearance. We still did not know his location, but Holmes quickly deduced that Franke, with Jenny's help, had faked his disappearance to escape his wife's hold. Soon after, we traded Franke for Jenny, who disappeared in sight of us. Her fate was unknown, with Holmes now focused on finding *her*, since he felt responsible for her current situation. Unlike Henry Franke, who'd simply run from his wife, Jenny's situation was not of her own making. Her mistakes were helping Franke, then lying when caught out. That all seemed simple enough, but several questions about her disappearance remained that I'd no answers for. I looked at Holmes, who was reading from his notebook.

'If Maximillian abducted Jenny, what could his motive be? To hand her over to Mr Greene so that he could take her back to his daughter?'

'That doesn't fit with the facts as we know them,' Holmes pointed out. 'And I would argue if Mrs Franke wanted Jenny to return, she would simply send her a message requesting it.'

'But why would she go?'

'To repair a relationship? To save her family and friends from Mrs Franke's vindictiveness? To atone for her mistakes. To harm Mrs Franke,' my friend said. 'That list of reasons is long.'

I frowned. I hadn't really considered any of that. 'What do you mean by "harm Mrs Franke"?'

Holmes inclined his head. 'There appears a genuine grief between them; exacerbated by *us*, true, and the probability is low, but given what we know *and* saw, we cannot rule it out.'

The thought of that poor innocent girl seeking a violent solution to her predicament seemed too fantastic a proposition.

Holmes then asked, 'Can you think of another reason someone might want to abduct Jenny?'

'Yes,' I replied. 'I'd hoped never to have to articulate it, but for a ransom?'

My friend nodded. 'And Jenny would probably have been worth a vast sum had I not ousted her. That is why I fear for her, Watson, because should these people discover Jenny has *no* value, they're likely to cut her throat.'

Sherlock Holmes turned to the window and said no more. The thought wasn't a pleasant one, and so I closed my eyes and relaxed, the train's motion rocking me into a pleasant unconsciousness, but no sooner had I reached that point of blissful ignorance, when I felt a light shake of my shoulder.

'It is time to wake up, Watson,' Holmes said. 'We arrive at Newark in ten minutes.'

The rest of the journey went fast as Holmes charmed a porter into helping us hire a carriage and driver. There were several to choose from, but we took the recommendation and, around thirty minutes later, were standing outside the neatly manicured landscape of a somewhat drearily signed entrance to

Maximillian's Park of Amusements.

We stood on a road that led under a mammoth rock-façade arched entrance. It appeared to blend in with the grey sky ahead of it, which felt intentional, perhaps to give an impression of some mystical opening to the park, which was entirely hidden behind a dense line of trees. My eyes fell on the two giant iron gates and I turned to Holmes.

'It's a little drab, don't you think?'

My friend shrugged. 'The aesthetic holds little interest for me, Watson. I've set my mind on more important matters. Now, let us head inside.'

I sighed. 'Hang on a minute. *If* we're to stay a night here,' I said, looking up at the light-grey sky, feeling the first drops of rain, 'we ought to find a hotel first.'

'There's one inside the park, Watson. And they're expecting us.'

'How did you achieve that?'

'I had Wiseman telegraph them yesterday to expect our arrival today. I knew you wanted to visit, so naturally I booked us ahead of time. Come on. We'll be lucky if we get into a pleasant room. I'm sure the place will be full by now.'

I shook my head and picked up my case.

Cornelius Mathias Maximillian had carefully designed his park to remain hidden amongst some of the largest trees I had ever seen, allowing for a contrived but stunning revelation. The vista I gaped at was quite an achievement because, despite what the entrance might have suggested, the inside was certainly *not* drab. In fact, I would go as far to say it was a veritable sea of vibrant colours and beautiful scenery, with rides I did not fully understand, along with the sweet smells of food, and... a serious lack of people.

'Where is everyone?' I asked the concierge as we entered the rather ostentatious three-story hotel, which – if you can believe it – had a giant wooden façade that was shaped like an octopus.

'It's the fall, sir,' the fellow said, tipping his hat and

practically shoving me inside.

Holmes was at the desk and had collected our key as I arrived. Our rooms were on the second floor. And after we'd settled, we were introduced to a young fellow named Liam Braiden, who was probably only twenty. His job, we discovered, was to guide visitors around the park, and I did not think for a moment we were being treated any differently to the other sporadic guests we occasionally saw, but it turned out that we were. Apparently, it only took living in opulence for a few days to spoil me.

Braiden had just finished taking us on a tour of the lower park, with its stunning gardens, painted scenery, and a rather attractive carousel with handcrafted wooden horses that several guests, along with their children, were enjoying riding in the very mild afternoon.

As we continued on the tour, the topic of our visit slipped into conversation, and that was when – to my initial surprise, and later amusement – Holmes had somehow given these fellows the false impression that I was *very* wealthy. Holmes was my agent, he'd said, assisting me to find a suitable investment that would not only return a profit, but would excite me – and investing in a "park of amusements" was top of that list, since one of my apparent close friends was a big contributor. Holmes did not reveal a name, and our young friend apparently understood why, as he tapped his nose and didn't broach the topic again. From that moment on, Braiden began politely making references about me in conversations, but did not speak directly to me. I played the part as best I could. Having someone talk *for* you, while you're actually stood there, was a strange feeling for me, but is apparently the norm amongst those I'd heard termed as the filthy rich.

'And here we come to the top of our bill, gentlemen. The sweet crust of the pie. Behold,' Braiden said in dramatic fashion, lifting his arms like a stage-hall actor and enticing us to be inspired by the wonder he presented. 'Maximillian's greatest achievement. The Punisher.'

'A rather good name, given how many injuries these

railway coasters inflict,' Holmes remarked coldly. The young man did not know how to respond to that. I was left with the impression that people were typically enthused when Braiden revealed The Punisher, as he'd intended, because it *was* an impressive sight – a considerably-sized structure of crisscrossed beams and rails. Holmes, however, was playing a role which not only confused the boy, but me also. Braiden's eyes widened, then he looked at me and quickly recovered. He shook his head, addressing the conversation directly with Holmes, and occasionally nodding reassuringly at me, as well. It was the most bizarre position Holmes had ever put me in.

'There were plenty of problems early on, but they're fixed now,' Braiden explained as we came to the side and could review the strange structure. 'This is a complete circuit, with front-facing cars, rather than awkward bench seats. They don't go fast enough to expel you like a cannon ball, but some people have occasionally suffered a broken bone, at worst, but usually just a bruise at most. Yet they still come.'

'And these rollercoasters are truly worthy of investment?' Holmes asked, his eyes taking in the entire structure.

'I think, if you didn't believe that, then you wouldn't be here,' Braiden suggested with misplaced confidence. Just then we heard a whistle and Liam Braiden frowned but excused himself to go and investigate.

Holmes gestured for us to follow, but instead of heading towards the entrance as Braiden had, Holmes navigated us through the people *leaving* the ride – the path being just wide enough for us to squeeze through – whose apparent enjoyment of the ride was supplanted by annoyance at us.

Leaving me to endure several looks of indignation, Holmes – who was simply ignoring everyone – almost caused a horrific scene when, quiet suddenly he dropped to his knee to collect something from the ground. Several people almost went over him, but at the last second, he stood and avoided the collision I was prepared for.

'What is it?' I asked, ignoring the stares.

'An odd sliver of wood.' Holmes then shoved it into his

pocket and indicated for me to follow him. The exit ramp led into the station through an arched, painted tunnel that widened significantly as it went further inside the building. The roof of the structure was made from glass, ensuring the station was well-lit during daylight hours. When we arrived alongside the track of the rollercoaster, I observed an empty train consisting five carriages each seating two persons. The station building was nicely decorated with murals depicting various scenes of railways around the world. It comprised one means of entrance and egress, with the entrance being longer to accommodate the queues of those waiting to ride. Despite so few people at the park, it appeared nearly all of them had lined up for The Punisher. When we reached the station entryway, I overserved a young oil-stained Irish operator who appeared distressed.

'What's wrong?' Braiden had asked as we arrived behind him.

'I lost a passenger, didn't I?' the young man said.

Braiden stared at him. 'What do you mean, *lost* a passenger? How do you lose a passenger?' he turned and jumped, perhaps because he wasn't expecting to find me standing behind him. His face turned almost purple. 'Oh no. Sir, you shouldn't be here. I'm sorry, perhaps you'd both be better off at the pavilion, where… hey,' he said, frowning at Holmes. 'What's he doing?'

We each turned to observe Holmes busily examining the train.

'You can't be doing that,' Braiden said, but Holmes ignored him.

My friend turned to the operator. 'You say missing. Do you mean he vanished into the air, or simply that he was missed?'

'Vanished, sir. Like magic.'

'Now I *must* protest!' Braiden grumbled, his demeanour becoming more uncertain, and even more so when Holmes turned a withering stare on him.

'I suggest you go and get the manager,' my friend demanded. 'We shall wait here while you do,'

Braiden considered his next move, looking between us as

he did so. He appeared lost for a moment, then he nodded and flew away.

Sherlock Holmes then smiled at the ride operator. 'Now we have some time,' he said, rubbing his hands together. 'Would you mind explaining what happened?' Holmes asked, opening his wallet and retrieving a five-dollar bill. 'If you *could* do so quickly and concisely, then I'll gladly hand you this bill.' The young operator, who we discovered was named Michael Ryan Byrne – an eighteen-year-old born of Irish immigrants – looked around before answering. On seeing the coast clear, and without further hesitation, he began his story.

'… and so, ten riders got on, but by God sir, I swear on my ma's life, only nine came off. One *was* missing. And I know it was Chip, sir, I swear it.'

My friend rubbed his chin in thought. 'I believe you. Chip?'

'Charles Murphy sir, a friend – well of sorts. He goes by Chip.'

'I see. And what was it that alerted you to his disappearance?'

Byrne frowned. 'Well, I didn't see him leave, sir, and I know he got on because he always sits in the same carriage.'

'Perhaps you just missed him leave?' my friend offered. 'It's easy enough to do. You were distracted and, in that time, Chip passed you by.'

The young man shook his head. 'But Chip rides this train at set times, sir. Always sits in the same rear carriage. Twice at ten, three times at noon. I could set my watch by it, he's that regular. Besides, there's no way *anyone* could miss him.'

Byrne's last statement caught Holmes's attention. 'And why is that?'

'Because Chip wears coloured outer garments, sir. Bright ones, too, *and* he's tall. Perhaps a little taller than you, sir? Most people like darker colours so he sticks out in a crowd.'

'Your observation skills impress me,' Holmes said.

'Thank you, but you don't have to take my word for it. *You* passed those people leaving to get to me,' the operator added.

'Did *you* see anyone dressed as I describe?'

Holmes grinned at the boy. 'I did not. Again, you impress me. What do you know about Chip Murphy?'

Byrne thought for a moment. 'He's an older gent, mid to late forties, perhaps? Bright orange hair and beard to match and pasty skin. A proper Irishman if ever you saw one.'

There was a certain look in my friend's eyes I knew so well. Holmes stayed animated by Byrne's conversation, and when he finished his story, Holmes handed over the fiver-dollar bill. To say young Byrne was pleased would be an understatement. Holmes had just handed him a week's money. Somehow, again, we'd arrived just in time to become involved in *another* disappearance, and just like with Jenny, it had happened within several feet of us.

Sherlock Holmes murmured for me to distract Byrne, and without pause I engaged him in conversation as Holmes, I could see, was examining the carriage this Murphy had apparently vanished from. I manoeuvred Byrne so his back was to Holmes, which enabled me to carry on a conversation and observe my friend at the same time, who was collecting and examining what appeared to be a sliver of wood, followed soon after by several slightly thicker fragments. Those he deposited into his pocket, replacing them with his lens, which he ran along every inch of the carriage. Once he'd collected several smaller samples, I saw him stand back and contemplate the ride. His eyes turned to me, as I loudly coughed. Braiden, I observed, was returning with the hotel manager.

Chapter Five

'I swear on the Bible, sir, Chip had vanished into the air.'

'Who the hell are you, and what are you doing snooping around my park?' the red-faced manager, a dangerous-looking Eddy Russell, asked Holmes.

'This is Mr Sherlock Holmes,' I said. 'A consulting—'

'Engineer,' Holmes interjected. 'From Great Britain.'

'A consulting *engineer*?' Russell said, the uncertainty clear in his voice. 'I never heard of no such thing, now—'

'Excuse me,' Holmes said, lifting a gloved hand, which stopped the manager in his tracks. 'If it helps, Mr Russell, I have a letter that not only details who I am but also why I'm here.' Holmes took a long, white envelope from his inside jacket pocket, and handed it to the manager, who snatched then opened it. Soon after, a look of surprise crossed his face. He folded the letter up and handed it back.

'Forgive me, sirs,' Russell said, his cheeks tinged a little red. 'If I had known…'

'You are aware now.'

Russell spread out his hand and then gave a nervous laugh, before leaning forward to Holmes and asking, 'What can I do to make this situation go away?'

'You can start by following any instructions I might give and allow Watson and me access to the park's rides – especially that interesting rollercoaster. Is that acceptable?'

'I don't see a problem with that,' Russell said.

'I'll need young Byrne's help too, since he understands its operation.'

'Agreed. Now I'll ask *you* for something in return. If there's some way to avoid calling in the police, I would consider it a favour.'

Holmes smiled. 'No crime appears to have been committed. I see no reason to call them.'

This news caused the manager to heave a sigh. 'Well, thank Mary and Joseph for that!'

Liam Braiden, who'd been examining the ride, came back to report his findings. 'Empty of anyone. There's nothing to account for his vanishing. Nothing.'

'So, where'd he go then?' Russell asked.

No one had an answer.

'If you'll excuse us,' Holmes said. 'Watson and I would like to take a stroll around the park, alone.'

Sherlock Holmes led me outside where the grey clouds had lifted, allowing the sun to brighten the day up immensely. We followed the path down to the entrance, and made our way over to that beautiful carousel, where Holmes indicated his intention to ride it, and naturally I followed.

We sat side by side as the operator sent us around. The smoothness of the mechanism that had us appearing to ride together surprised me.

'We can talk here,' Holmes said.

'What was in that letter?'

'A precaution which worked to our advantage,' Holmes said. 'It's from Maximillian. He gives them out to prospective investors.'

'And he gave one to you?'

My friend smiled. 'Not quite. I acquired one he'd already

written, then adjusted it for my needs.'

I gasped. 'You *forged* it?'

'I *adjusted* it,' Holmes corrected. 'To include us both and give us time, should we need it.'

'And what if they should ask him?' I asked, concerned we might find trouble from it.

Holmes appeared indifferent. 'Mr Greene will curtail any need for us to explain anything.'

'Unless he uses it to get rid of *us*?' I countered.

'Unlikely. Greene needs us to persuade his son-in-law never to return.'

I thought for a moment. '*If* we ever find him.'

'There is that,' Holmes agreed. 'But this fellow Russell, he strikes me as a man who knows a thing or two about people disappearing.'

I frowned. 'What did you see in him?'

'A deep mistrust of strangers he hides poorly behind that bushy moustache and fat cigar. The fellow holds its so tight because his hands shake so violently. I suspect there's much more going on at this park than Russell might want revealed, and we must be careful not to, because *if* Greene is a financial backer, we should be cautious about how much involvement he might have in this business.'

'Meaning he could have sanctioned some nefarious activity?'

'Or unwittingly supported it, because it makes a huge profit, and he turns a blind eye to how that revenue is made.' Holmes smiled. 'So, we don't want to expose anything, especially to him, that we cannot prove.'

'Understood.' I remained thoughtful for a time. 'And you believe he's involved in this fellow Chip's disappearance?'

'He plays some part, I am sure. What size that role is remains unknown. So we will watch and pay attention. I don't suppose you noticed the gardeners?'

'Rough-looking fellows,' I said.

'They're convicts, I believe. Most of them.'

I nodded. 'Escapees, or recently released?'

'Whimsey might suggest the recently released, but experience suggests otherwise. We cannot know for certain, but this location is about as remote as we've seen. Remote, here, often means lawlessness. We should be on alert.'

'And what of Jenny?'

'One problem at a time, Watson. If Jenny is here, we'll find her. But let's investigate this interesting puzzle on the rollercoaster first.'

I sighed. 'It seems unlikely to be a fluke that on the day we arrive, another person disappears under *impossible* circumstances.'

'Yes, all these things are connected. Our client, his brother and sister-in-law, her father, the girl Jenny – and this Maximillian appears central to them all,' Holmes said, offering me a cigarette. We both shared a match. 'We must tread carefully. If this Russell is clever, he'll have already interpreted my interrupting you before as he should, which was to stop you from giving him the information that would likely have had us murdered in our beds. He is smart, Watson, and therefore I played a hand that might have served us better down the road: Maximillian's letter. It might be enough to keep us alive, but I should be grateful if you'd keep your old revolver handy.'

I hadn't told Holmes I was carrying it. 'I just had a premonition to bring it. How did you know?'

'Your jacket's balance is off.'

Of course. 'We appear to be the catalyst for ridiculous situations lately,' I remarked, chuckling. 'What do you make of this latest disappearance?'

'Well, of course, as you rightly pegged it, it would be impossible for anyone to leave a ride *before* it reached the station, without them suffering a significant injury or worse – and were that the case, there would be evidence of it – but as you heard Liam say, after an inspection of the ride, Murphy was nowhere to be found. It *is* a conundrum, Watson. Where could this fellow have gone?'

'I know that's important,' I said. 'But I feel compelled to

point out again that we came here in search of Jenny, and I believe she should remain our priority.'

Sherlock Holmes put a hand on my shoulder. 'I understand, Watson. I'm worried about her too. But so far, I've seen nothing suggesting Jenny is here. Her abductors might have reason to be cautious, but those others here may have seen something, and they'll be more likely give that up with the right persuasion.'

'Coin?'

Holmes nodded. 'The best kind. I made a visual inspection of the keys and took a peek at the register to see if there were any inconsistences. They *appear* to match, but we cannot know for certain. There aren't many people here, which should make it easier if we have to review the empty rooms – but something tells me that Jenny isn't in the hotel.'

'You think they may have her tied up somewhere?' I said, my agitation growing.

Holmes sighed. 'As I pointed out before, Watson – if they realise her true value, then in all likelihood she may already have been dispatched.'

'I hope to God you're wrong,' I grumbled.

'There is some hope,' Holmes added. 'It is *slight*, but I believe if the circumstances are right, we might still find her alive.'

'Here?'

'If not here, then somewhere,' Holmes said. I did not feel reassured.

When our ride came to a halt, I followed Holmes off the carousel and we ambulated toward that massive rollercoaster with its missing man.

'Do you have any idea where this Chip might have gone to?'

My friend gave me a sideways look. 'Several, but before we get to them, I should like to review the train he was sitting in, one last time.'

When we reached the entrance to The Punisher, we greeted Michael Byrne, who welcomed us back. That five-dollar bill had kept him very loyal. Byrne invited us into a private room where he'd just boiled a kettle of water and was making tea – apparently, his Irish family had instilled that tradition in him. Byrne handed us a tin cup of hot milky tea, and we perched on high stools to drink them.

'Can you tell me anything else you know about Chip?' Holmes asked. 'The smallest details can help us.'

'I don't know a lot. He's been here a little under a month. He was hired to look after the facilities, and he's done a good job as far as I know. Keeps all them parts and other things we need in stock.'

'And who hired him?'

'That was Eddy, I reckon. I could be wrong, though.'

'Does he have any background you're aware of?'

Byrne shook his head. 'Chip's a real private man. He never told me much of nothing. Me and Liam thought he was probably hiding from something because these fellows often slipped into the country without the right papers.'

'Ahh, I see. And what gave you that impression?'

Byrne took a mouthful of tea. 'He could be as jumpy as a cat.'

'In what way?'

'If you came on him suddenly and without warning, and he didn't hear you? That would make him *very* nervous. It wasn't unusual to see or hear him drop something because of it.'

'Indeed,' Holmes said, smiling. 'And you know little beyond his arrival here?'

'Not really. If he told anyone, it'd probably be Eddy. They seemed close.'

'No family you're aware of?'

'Chip has family, sir. I know that. He often talked about seeing his old ma. He visits most weekends.'

Holmes finished his tea in thought, then placed the cup on a tray. 'A highly strung young man quick to annoy, is Chip?'

Byrne shook his head. 'No, sir. He's older, probably your age? Cool headed in a crisis. Hardly *anything* bothered him... well until this morning, that is.'

'What happened this morning?' I asked.

'Some rough-looking men arrived and Chip said they were trouble. I know he talked to Eddy about them.'

'You saw them?'

Byrne nodded. 'Brutish-looking. Iron workers, or so they said. Three of them. Heavy build. Dirty looking. Two had large moustaches, the other was clean shaven. They were dressed more like lumberjacks.'

I looked to Holmes, who acknowledged me with raised eyebrows. Byrne had given a pretty accurate description of the men we'd also seen emerging from that streetcar in New York.

'They'd come looking for work, so one said,' Byrne continued, 'but Eddy didn't like the looks of them, or something. They were gone by the time you arrived.'

My friend stared at his feet apparently lost in thought. He then turned to Byrne. 'And Chip remained concerned about them, even once they'd gone?' he asked.

'It certainly seemed so. Chip stayed as far away from them as he could. It was obvious he was avoiding them.'

'But did he seem *unusually* worried?'

Byrne shrugged. 'He seemed more nervous, than worried, but I never saw him either way before so I might be misreading him.'

Holmes smiled. 'You appear a pretty observant fellow, that bodes well for us! And when these men left, did Chip begin to relax, or did he remain on alert?'

'He was definitely jumpy. I could tell he wasn't the same. Chip rides The Punisher frequently. He couldn't seem to get enough of it. But today when he boarded, he just sat there looking down at his hands until the train pulled out. It was as if he knew something bad was going to happen. I thought there was *something* wrong, sir. And when the train came back, and he wasn't on it…I all but died.'

'You did not see him in the carriage when it came back into the station?'

Byrne shook his head adamantly. 'No sir. Admittedly, my initial focus was on the front carriages while I applied the brake. Once the train was locked, I looked back towards the rear to make sure all the passengers got off – it wasn't unusual to have one pass out on the ride – just as I always did, and I swear on the Bible, sir, Chip had vanished into the air.'

It was not the first time we'd heard *that* idiom over the past few days. Holmes then asked, 'What is the ride's duration?'

'One minute, eighteen seconds, sir.'

Holmes stepped onto the track. 'The track runs through this tunnel first?'

'Right. We added that recently. It's just darkened up, no scenery. Coming out of the darkness causes a momentary disorientation which adds to the thrill.'

'I see. And how long is the train in this tunnel for?'

'Twenty-five seconds, sir.'

'And could anyone leave the train and return to the platform whilst in motion in this tunnel?'

'Not easily. The platform is really small and would require jumping onto. Even *if* anyone managed it, when they came out, they'd walk right by me. I stand at the entrance.'

'I see. But a person could also leave in the direction the train is travelling?'

'Well yes sir, they *could*, but the platform doesn't go all the way. There's a curve to the track, and the tunnel width decreases as the train comes out. It would be difficult to jump out inside the tunnel, almost impossible once the train exits. The track is built on a platform, sir. The mouth of the tunnel is fifteen feet *off* the ground.'

'A difficult task, I agree, but not an impossible one. Certainly not if you'd ridden the ride a hundred times."

'Yes, but Liam also talked to the other passengers. None said they saw anyone attempting to leave the train.'

Holmes nodded. 'True, but haven't you already explained *why* no one would notice him?'

Byrne looked confused. 'Sir?'

'Well, surely, if this disorientation coming out of the tunnel is as great as you suggest, then that could explain why? But we mustn't forget Chip, you said, always rode in the rear carriage.'

'That is true, sir. He never varied it,' Byrne said, his confusion still clear.

'Then I take you at your word,' Holmes replied kindly. 'Tell me then, in your experience, do many people turn and look behind them when enjoying this ride?'

Our young friend appeared surprised. 'No, I suppose not.'

Holmes nodded. 'But, should anyone successfully leave the train, and exit *away* from the tunnel, would you see them leave?'

'No, sir, I wouldn't. But it's impossible.'

'Improbable, I agree, but *not* impossible.' Holmes appeared pleased. We followed him back to the rear of the train, where he stepped inside the carriage. 'All that remains now is for me to experience the ride itself.'

I admit I was a little envious as I watched Holmes's carriage disappear into the tunnel. I then realised the importance of the glass roof. It not only gave us our light, but from the engineer's platform, we had an unobstructive view of the train as it went over the track. At length, the train returned to the station and Michael applied the break. As I approached Holmes, who was still seated in his carriage, he turned to me, his expression was unreadable as usual, but I noticed his cheeks were tinged red,

'How was it?' I asked, as my friend stepped out and collected his hat and cane.

Holmes momentarily dropped his façade. 'It was exhilarating, Watson,' he whispered excitedly. 'Certainly worth a bruise or two. The forces experienced aren't just impressive, they're quite literally terrifying. But better than that, I believe I now know how Chip disappeared.' Holmes then tapped my chest and his stoic expression returned as young Byrne approached us. 'Well, thank you, Michael. That was most informative. I should like to look at Chip's room, if that's possible?'

Byrne nodded. 'I'll take you right now, since my ride is closed.'

When we stepped into the bright afternoon sunshine, Holmes stopped us from going any further, asking us to wait until he had finished examining the exit. He then ran his lens along portions of the exit lane and collected more of those odd splinters. He lifted them to his lens and examined each for several seconds. Whatever they once were, they appeared to excite him. When Holmes finished, Michael Byrne walked us to the hotel and collected the key to the missing Charles "Chip" Murphy's room from Eddy Russell, who replaced Byrne as our guide, and accompanied us to the missing employee's room.

* * *

'I understand you sent several iron workers away who came looking for work?' Holmes said, as we reached the doorway of Murphy's room. Russell went to open the door, but Holmes prevented him from doing so. 'I need just a moment,' he said, dropping to a knee and running his lens along the wood.

'Answering your question, there's nothing to that. We get people looking for work frequently,' Russell said. 'They think it'll be an easy place to work. It ain't. It requires dedication and long hours, plus you need a certain *something* when dealing with the public. A spark. A friendly demeanour... but those two men would frighten our guest away.'

Holmes looked up. 'Two, you say?'

'Well, yes, what of it?'

'Byrne suggested there were three.'

Russell looked momentarily unsure, then his expressed became neutral. 'He counted wrong, that's all.'

My friend nodded. 'I appreciate you clearing that point up. Let me ask you something. Had you ever felt you'd seen these men before?'

Russell appeared to think about that. 'I *did* get a little feeling I might have. I often see many people during a day, but unless they're regular enough to recall, I'm never really sure where I've seen them. You think they'd been here before, and I just forgot it?'

'It would certainly seem possible,' Holmes said. 'I know

little about them, but from what Michael said, I believe they came looking for someone, and they possibly found him.'

'Meaning Chip?'

Holmes nodded.

Russell frowned. 'Well, what's their game, then?'

My friend tapped his lens on his lips for a few moments, then turned to us and smiled. 'I have several theories,' he said.

'Should I send a message to Max and let him know what's happening?'

Holmes shook his head. 'We'll report back when we see him tomorrow. Now *this* is interesting,' he said, turning his lens to the lock. 'Someone clearly forced this door open, but it then appears to have been carefully locked up afterwards.' Holmes turned to the manager. 'Perhaps you'd be kind enough to open it now?'

Russell nodded, then opened the room, and we all gasped at the disarray. Holmes continued examining the lock. 'Curious. The wood around the lock was splintered, but if you'll notice, it was then squashed back into place when the door was subsequently locked, which means it was done so pretty soon *after* this,' he said, gesturing towards the room.

'It's safe to suggest someone came looking for something they thought Chip had?' I offered.

Holmes nodded, but said nothing, preferring to remain fixed in position at the door, his eyes constantly moving. He then turned a smile to me. 'It's quite remarkable.'

'Horrendous, more like it!' Russell moaned. 'I suppose we'll have no choice but to call the police now, eh?'

Holmes turned to him. 'We really don't know enough. I doubt they'll have any more idea why this happened than you.'

Russell nodded, but I couldn't help noticing he seemed relieved. 'What do you make of it?' he asked.

'Well, as Watson alluded to, *someone* had a reason to do this,' Holmes said.

'That much is obvious,' blurted out Russell. 'Those fellows *ransacked* his place. Do you think they found what they were looking for?'

'I do not,' Holmes answered. There was a sparkle in his eyes. 'I think Chip outsmarted them.'

Russell frowned. 'Explain?'

'When they examined his room, I believe they found it as it appears now.'

Russell gasped. 'You mean this is someone else's doing?'

Sherlock Holmes shook his head. 'Chip did this himself.'

'How can you possibly know that?' Russell asked him. There was no missing his irritation.

'There are plenty of clues to suggest it. The locked door, for one, this mess, another. Add to it Chip's eventual disappearance, and one might conceive of the basket from just one weave.'

'You don't sound like any engineer *I* ever spoke with before,' Eddy Russell said – the accusation in his voice unmistakable. 'I think it's time you came clean with me,' he added menacingly.

Chapter Six

'Well, thinking and talking ain't gonna get nothing done, not around here.'

Sherlock Holmes clasped his hands behind his back and smiled. 'I've credited you with a modicum of intelligence, Mr Russell, so let's not bandy words. It has been clear for some time I am *not* an engineer.'

'True,' Russell said. 'So, just who *are* you then?'

'I am a *consulting* detective, from London.'

Russell stared at him. 'I don't know what that means.'

'Mr Holmes solves crimes,' I said. 'He's *world* famous.' Rather than having the intended effect, it appeared to confuse Russell's more.

'You're the police?'

Holmes shook his head. 'I am a private consultant, Mr Russell. I am *paid* to solve puzzles.'

'But not paid by Max?' Russell said, narrowing his eyes. 'I'd know if that was the case.'

'No,' Holmes replied. 'I am not retained by Max.'

'Mr Greene, then?' Russell furtively asked.

'I *cannot* confirm that,' my friend said cleverly.

'But you're *not* denying it, either.' Russell appeared to relax.

'Well, if you're taking Mr Greene's dollars, then you do have friends high in the world! I had you pegged a journalist, but you sure make a lot more sense to me now.'

'I appreciate that compliment,' Holmes said.

'You've seen something?' I asked, coming beside them. Russell, I noticed, was decidedly nervous. 'Something in this room?'

'Look at it for a moment, Watson. Tell me what *you* see?'

'I see an upside-down room.'

Holmes nodded. 'That's an obvious and predictable answer, Watson; look *harder*. Realise the room in your mind and picture how a fellow might choose to go about searching it. Follow them as they enact it, and once you have these images, tell me, do you notice *anything* now that might strike you as odd?'

I struggled to see anything beyond the haphazard array of items around the room. Holmes had seen something, but I simply could not fathom what. The answer was right in front of me, but my mind went blank. Seconds later, I noticed *one* oddity. I gave a voice to it. 'None of the furniture appears to have been touched.'

'Bravo, my dear friend. And your conclusion?'

'They knew what they were looking for?'

Holmes shook his head. 'If they knew that, why leave the room in this state and carefully lock it afterwards? Think harder. The room is in disarray, but in a particular way. Look at the furniture. Not *one* item appears molested. No doors opened. No drawers riffled through.' Holmes went to the wardrobe cabinet and opened it to reveal clothes hanging. The drawers inside he opened and reviewed one by one. 'Interesting,' Holmes said. I slipped in beside him and observed the last drawer. It contained undergarments, each folded very neatly.

'Perhaps someone disturbed them?' Russell asked as he leant against the doorframe.

Holmes shook his head. 'No. No one has been in this room between the time he locked it, and we found it. It was a smart move on Chip's part, since *anyone* who came to examine it could never be certain if what they sought hadn't already been taken.'

'You're convinced Chip did this?' I asked.

'The evidence strongly suggests it.'

'But *why*? Why would he do this himself?' Russell asked.

'He appeared to *have* a good reason,' Holmes said, turning his eyes to Russell. 'You're sure you can't answer why?'

'Me?' Russell looked indignantly at Holmes. 'Why should I have that answer?'

Holmes returned to the wardrobe. 'Because I don't believe you've been completely truthful with us.'

'Really? Because you know me so well?' Russell growled.

Holmes turned. 'My apologies. Mr Russell, I intended no offence. It was my understanding people from America enjoyed frankness.'

Russell gave a nervous chuckle. 'And you sure *are* frank.'

My friend nodded. 'It can be time saving.' He remained quiet for a time, then rubbed his lip as he thought. 'It's sloppy and amateurish, but good enough for his purposes.'

'To buy himself time?' I asked.

Holmes smiled at me. 'Yes, and I suspect I know what for.'

'How are you so sure Chip did this?' Russell asked. He wasn't taking anyone's word for anything.

'The floor is littered with rubbish – trash – from that empty wastepaper basket. There are footprints outside his door, consistent with the descriptions of your visitors. But there is enough exposed carpet within to tell me they did not enter. I suspect Chip forced the lock to give the impression the room was broken into. He then emptied the basket over the floor and bed, added a few items of low worth, some of which he broke, all to suggest that someone had searched his room. He then exited and – out of habit – *locked* the door afterwards.'

'So the locked door was the clue?' Russell asked.

'That was one factor, yes.'

'Chip may have been clever,' I said. 'But it appears to me he might rely on a little luck as well, because he couldn't have known they *wouldn't* search his room?'

'Ah, but that's the beauty of it, Watson. It wouldn't have changed the outcome had they done so. And we know his charade worked, because it does appear he misdirected these fellows into believing *another* group had possibly removed their prize. Do you follow now?'

I did, and said so.

Sherlock Holmes said nothing after that. He stood scrutinising the floor while Eddy Russell paced behind us. Eventually, Holmes's inaction appeared the last straw of patience for the manager, who finally lost his cool.

'Forgive my impatience. But in God's own name, *why* are you just staring at the floor, man?'

'I am thinking,' Holmes said.

'Well, *thinking* and *talking* ain't gonna get *nothing* done, not around here. This place is hard, Mr Holmes. These people, the workers, they require a lot of attention. Losing one of their own is pretty painful. Finding Chip is my priority. I say we look for where he went.'

Holmes turned to Russell and nodded. 'Yes, an excellent idea. Close the park and ensure no one leaves. Then rally all your staff and go search it, he's bound to turn up!'

Eddy Russell seemed *far* happier being given *that* task. 'I'll get on to it. Just lock that room when you're done and bring me the key.'

'I shall do as you say,' Holmes said. When Russell had left, Holmes quietly closed the door and sat on the missing Charles Murphy's bed.

* * *

'Will they be successful?'

Sherlock Holmes shook his head and then lit his pipe. 'Chip is long gone. No one will find him now.' I could tell his mind was on the problem at hand.

'And Jenny?'

'I am hopeful. This mobilisation helps us, because although I do not expect Chip to be found, the action to search for him may uncover *her*, or possibly a clue to finding her.'

'Two birds with one stone, eh?'

'Precisely.'

I nodded. 'The description of those men seems awfully familiar, Holmes.' This caused him to turn to me.

'Yes, *we* narrowly escaped them in New York. I admit I wasn't expecting to find them here, and certainly not before us. I'm missing…something. These men, I firmly believe, work for Maximillian. Does it seem right, then, that this Russell doesn't know them?'

I considered that while Holmes smoked furiously.

'No. I suppose we need to decide exactly what their motives are,' I suggested.

'And work from there?' Holmes nodded. 'It's not your worst idea, Watson.'

I chuckled. 'Were these men present when Jenny disappeared?'

My friend nodded. 'At least one. I recognised him when we boarded that streetcar. I also believe Maximillian, or someone close to him, set those men on the path ahead of us deliberately. That's *how* they reached a streetcar before we did.'

'Well, we know at least *three* people with means and the motive to want to hire them,' I said. 'The Frankes *or* Mr Greene.'

'There is a fourth. Jenny,' Holmes said.

'You can't be serious?'

'Whilst it might appear unlikely, we cannot rule her out. Not until we find something that gives us a reason to.'

'She's fourteen, Holmes.'

'Good-natured people, even children, have fooled us both before,' my friend said, rubbing his chin in thought.

'Fair enough, but she's *hardly* a master criminal.'

'But could possibly be working for one,' my friend pointed out.

When it came to sentimental or emotional topics, inevitably we'd end them by disagreeing. As I did not want to cause an argument, I elected to remain quiet. Holmes didn't necessarily see how cold he could come across, especially when in the thick of a case. I should point out also that Sherlock Holmes routinely failed to attach any emotional context to the scenarios he envisaged.

"It is useless to attribute emotional connection to simple facts, which are inanimate pieces of an incomplete puzzle," he once said to me.

"But what if those facts determine if a person is found dead, or alive?" I had asked. "Surely, then, they'd have an emotional context?"

My friend simply shook his head. "Facts are the truth *about* events, Watson, as opposed to an interpretation of them. Out of context, those facts mean nothing. Why therefore would anyone attribute emotion to them?"

I never found a suitable answer – at least not one Holmes would accept.

'This thing *is* illusive, Watson,' Holmes said, exhaling another blue cloud into an already heavy room. 'These occurrences depend upon a connection we are yet to uncover. One thing *is* clear, however. These problems *are* linked and it would appear Maximillian is at its core.'

* * *

Sherlock Holmes collected several items of interest from Chip Murphy's room, including a small carved wooden flower – which appeared to have broken off something larger. Several samples of ash, a few of those slivers of wood, along with some fragments of blue paper – mixed in with that rather extensive pile of rubbish covering the living space – were placed into a selection of small white envelopes by Holmes.

'We still have to explain *how* Chip left that train. From what you said earlier, it seems more likely he jumped out of the tunnel and fled.'

'That *is* a plausible answer, Watson, and one I had given serious consideration to, until I found these,' said Holmes, holding up one of those slivers of wood. 'I've found them in several locations, and I now believe I know what they are, and how they were used – and it gives me a somewhat more interesting answer. Chip Murphy *vanished* from that train, Watson, and it's unlikely anyone will ever see him again.'

My heart sank. 'He's dead then?'

'He vanished,' Holmes corrected.

'I don't wish to contradict you, Holmes,' I said. 'But people *don't* just vanish. You said so yourself.'

Holmes offered me a smile. 'Correct. So, what's the answer, then?'

I thought hard about the situation, then I clicked my fingers and laughed, because the solution seemed so obvious.

'You have it?' Holmes asked.

'I believe so. It's all to do with those men, isn't it? *They* got to him first!'

'Good. Explain,' Holmes said.

'Russell said he saw two men, but Michael said there *were* three. It's so obvious I don't understand why I didn't see it before. They'd *already* disposed of Chip, and one who looked somewhat similar in build and height, et cetera, took his place *on* the train?'

'Nicely reasoned,' Holmes said, clapping his hands together. 'You know, you really do habitually undersell your abilities, Watson. But I didn't hear your explanation of how this fellow left the station unobserved.'

'Oh, that's easy,' I replied. I was in my stride now. 'He just hid himself down in the crowd.'

'Well, well. *Sometimes* the obvious answer *is* the correct solution,' my friend said, chuckling.

'I've solved it, then?' I cried.

Sherlock Holmes gave me a look which paused my exultation. Then he smiled. 'Actually, Watson, almost everything you just said was erroneous, but I am grateful you're *attempting* to use your brain to *think*,' Holmes said.

I sighed. 'And I do so appreciate your encouragement, Holmes,' I replied as sarcastically as it was meant. 'Do you have the solution, then?' I asked.

There was the faintest smile on my friend's face as he held up one of those silvers of wood. 'This little thing forms part of the solution,' he said.

* * *

'Then search the place again!' We heard Russell's yelling before we got to his office – he was that loud – just in time to see Liam with the sense to scuttle away. Holmes tapped my shoulder and pointed, and I followed him inside.

'Oh, it's you, Mr Holmes,' Russell said in apparent disapproval. 'We haven't found Chip yet. We're still looking though.'

'Here are Chip's keys,' he said, dropping them onto the table. 'I believe there is nothing to be gained by reviewing his room any further. Now, in order for me to answer why it was necessary to manufacture this elaborate escape, I have *one* question. Did you hire Chip, or did Maximillian?'

Russell narrowed his eyes. 'Why do you need to know that?'

Holmes maintained a relaxed expression. 'I prefer *all* the facts about a case, especially when I'm prepared to present them to the official police.'

Russell stood. 'Now, you just wait a darn minute.'

'Do you have anything to add that might mitigate your involvement?'

The fellow's face turned almost purple. 'What the devil do you mean accusing me?'

'I advise you to speak now...'

Sherlock Holmes had suggested earlier that the park manager held some nefarious position in Maximillian's company, and whereas Maximillian *might* be a kingpin in New York, Russell it seemed was shaping himself to become New Jersey's equivalent. After we'd finished searching Chip's room for clues, Holmes told me he intended to push Eddy Russell as far as he could, in hopes he might reveal *something* about the other activities of the park. From the way the fellow was sweating, I thought Holmes's gamble was paying off. Eddy Russell slumped into his chair, looking up with wild eyes I didn't like the look of.

'Shut the door, Watson,' Holmes said.

I quickly obeyed.

'Now, Mr Russell. Time is short. If you confess everything to me now, I promise on my word as an English gentleman you will get a fair trial. Attempt to deceive me, and I will crush you like a bug. Are we clear?'

'You don't know who you're playing with,' Russell said, leaning towards the desk, his hands reaching for something under the table. I revealed my revolver, cocked it, and aimed the barrel at Russell's head. 'Hands on the table, please.'

Eddy Russell licked his lips as he stared at me. Holmes soon added to his grief by pushing the tip of his cane into the fellow's neck, causing him to kick his chair back to escape, but only succeeded in wedging himself against the wall, where he remained pinned by Holmes's cane.

My friend demanded Russell settle, but the fellow still had some fight in him. When it appeared as though he was about to launch a counterattack – despite looking into the barrel of my revolver – Holmes shook his head. 'There is a spring-loaded knife inside this cane, Mr Russell, the tip of which you must surely feel? *If* I release it, that blade will puncture your carotid artery.' This appeared to settle him. Holmes turned to me. 'Doctor, how long would this fellow have if I punctured his carotid?'

Russell turned his eyes to me, the evil purpose in them replaced now with fear. I knew Holmes had no intention of killing the man, and yet, I admit, the coldness by which he'd asked that question caused *me* discomfort.

'Minutes,' I said, not breaking eye contact.

'Minutes…,' Holmes echoed, turning to Russell and pushing his cane a little harder to further his point.

That was when the fellow collapsed, and told us everything…

* * *

'He's an escaped convict,' Russell said. 'They *all* are. They make it to some place in New York, and are given food and new clothes, then if they're lucky they get sent up here. Some remain in New York, working for Max. None of them have real names, not anymore. They're just faces now. Those that don't leave after a few days mostly look after the grounds. They're peaceful folk who just had a bad lot. Those who seek violence usually find it, and they're dealt with. We have to be careful because for obvious reason they're off any records. The local bailiff *might* check on us, but Max has him pretty subdued.'

Sherlock Holmes had removed his cane from Russell's neck and was now sat on the edge of his desk. I kept him covered, but it appeared as though any fight he might have made had all but been quashed. 'I see. So, Maximillian can continue *rehabilitating* these convicts and immigrants with no records, for a profit, I assume?'

Eddy Russell sighed as he nodded.

'And you operate in this isolation with impunity, since there are barely enough policemen in Newark to cover the town's population, let alone an amusement park an hour away.'

'The park manages its own security. It's all agreed with the constable.'

'I see. And how many men *does* the constable have anyway? Fifteen? Twenty?'

Russell appeared surprised. 'You seem to know everything.'

'I am a very thorough man, Mr Russell. I am also an observant one. You have a tattoo on your right arm you keep well hidden, but when you fold your arms, enough of it is revealed under your rolled up shirt cuff to present a style I recognise from my many hours of looking at convict photographs and reading descriptions, when engaged on several cases with the Pinkertons…Ah, I see you recognise them?'

Russell said nothing.

'You've been incarcerated, haven't you?'

'I did time. I paid with sweat and blood.' Russell slumped a little, then took in a breath. 'Listen, Mr Holmes. Max pays me to keep these fellows in check, and that's what I do.'

'By overlooking his and their acts of lawlessness?'

'Sure. But a fellow *deserves* a fresh start, doesn't he?'

Holmes shrugged. 'I might agree, if he's paid his debts to society, like you appear to have. But the authorities will eventually catch those who are running. That isn't my concern. You picking which laws you'll follow is. Now, what was Chip's real name?'

'I don't know. I swear on Mary's name. They come. They sometimes work. They eventually leave. Sometimes on a horse, or in a box. That's all I know. What else do you *want* from me, mister?'

Holmes stood, then gestured for me to holster my revolver. He turned to the less anxious manager. 'Do you know where Chip fled to?'

Russell shook his head. 'If I knew I'd tell.'

Sherlock Holmes nodded. 'I believe you.'

Russell sighed. 'What happens now?'

'Now?' Holmes said, standing. 'You're going to tell me who those men were, and what they were really doing.'

'They came to… collect someone,' Russell said, sighing.

The skin around Holmes's jaw went taunt. 'Was it a girl?'

Russell closed his eyes and nodded.

Holmes stepped away from the desk. His expression unreadable. 'Take me to where they were holding her, this instant.'

* * *

'Yes, this is blood,' I said, looking up at Russell from the floor of the room he'd shown us to. The revulsion on my face couldn't have been clearer. 'Fortunately for you, it's a superficial amount.'

I stood and moved aside as Holmes began an examination of the carpet and its stain.

'There's more on this bed,' my friend said, and then pointed to the wall. 'And there, you see these odd marks? Screw holes, Watson. Something was attached here.' Holmes cast his eyes around the wall, then smiled and pulled a bell-rope which was attached to a false panel on what we thought was a chimney. I held the rope while Holmes retrieved the items from within.

I looked at Russell, who, I might add, was as shocked as we were.

'Shackles,' I said. 'Good God, those brutes held her against her will!'

'Wait a moment,' Holmes interrupted. He was frowning. His expression suggested he'd discovered something that he wasn't expecting. 'You said earlier these fellows came to *collect* this girl?'

'That's right.'

My friend's frown deepened. 'How long had she been here?'

'Almost a week.'

'Then it wasn't *our* missing girl,' I said, almost sighing my relief. That was until I realised there might be another girl in danger.

Holmes stared at the room for a while long, then nodded. He turned a disgusted look at Russell. '*This* is wrong, sir.'

Russell looked ashamed, but offered no explanation. Before I could ask anything, Holmes said, 'Thank you for your time.' He then turned and left. I chose not to acknowledge the fellow at all and quickly trailed after Holmes.

It was late-afternoon, and the kitchen would begin making preparations for dinner. I was hungry, but was told to expect food in maybe two and a half or possibly three hours. My experiences to date at this rather grotesque hotel were becoming intolerable and not for the first time I silently wished we were back in New York. All this went through my mind as I followed Holmes back to our room. After we entered, he sighed and threw himself into the chair.

I sat beside him. 'What is it?'

'I've miscalculated,' my friend eventually said. 'For a *second* time.'

'To do with this girl?'

'This *place*, you mean.' Holmes sat up. 'I know this might come as an inconvenience, my dear fellow, but it is imperative we leave the park and head back to New York.'

'Holmes, I go where you go,' I replied.

My friend squeezed my shoulder. 'Then pack your things. We have a long ride, and I believe if we use Byrne's services to the station, we'll arrive in plenty of time to catch the six-fifteen to the New Jersey terminal.'

'What do you intend to do about Russell?'

'I believe Mr Russell's transgressions will shortly catch him up,' Holmes said. 'America has its problems, Watson, but we must give them time. They're still in their infancy when it comes to a robust prison system. These places are overcrowded, Watson, with conditions ripe for disease. Those given life rarely serve their full term.'

'It sound awful, yet law-abiding citizens should be protected. If it's as bad as you say, it should be more of a deterrent.'

'Yes, but America is so large, that should those inmates find a way to escape, and if they move centrally across the country and away from larger coastal cities, they're unlikely to ever be caught.'

'What can we do then?' I asked.

'Nothing. We have no legal standing or status the Newark constable might recognise. A man, I might add, who is possibly funded by Maximillian. Sadly, if we are to maintain our own liberty, we *must* walk away.'

'And we're going to just let it continue?' I didn't care for that.

Holmes shook his head. 'Of course not. I have contacts in New York. One is a Pinkerton, Watson. We'll lay it *all* before him, and he can decide how he wants to approach it. We may need his help, if we're to find Jenny.'

I felt a lot better about that. 'And you're sure it *wasn't* Jenny in that room?'

'Yes. I believe Russell was telling the truth about that.'

'Well, he might be a despicable villain, Holmes, who absolutely deserves time behind bars, but I also didn't get the impression he was lying. In fact, I think the evidence of that room appalled him, as much as it did me.'

Holmes gave a slow nod. 'He clearly knows what the workers use that room for, but my observations of the man suggest he wouldn't partake. There was evidence of multiple girls, who appear a perk for those convicts.'

'That's disgusting, Holmes.'

'I told you Maximillian was an odious man.'

'True. And I'd recognise a den of iniquity in *any* country,' I said. 'But the blood tells me some of these poor women might possibly have been hurt.'

Holmes gave me a sad smile. 'Abused, *and* paid for it.'

I had no response.

'And now we've discovered this place, with all its oddities, I recognise the truth. I've made a grievous error, Watson. One that might ensure an outcome I rather hoped would remain uncertain.'

'Are you talking about Jenny?'

Holmes nodded. 'She isn't here. I expected to find her. That's *why* we must return. Someone has outplayed me.'

'You don't seem that upset about it,' I pointed out.

Holmes shrugged. 'Someone outsmarted me, Watson. Twice. I'm not happy about it, but the challenge it presents is…stimulating.'

I shook my head. Sherlock Holmes could be a very odd man. 'What about Chip? Do you think he really *was* a criminal on the run?'

'The facts support it,' Holmes said. 'He was jumpy, distrustful, and quick to scare. All valid reason to fear being caught, especially when strangers arrive.'

'And when he needed to escape,' I said. 'He chose that elaborate means to go about it. I still believe he'd need help to accomplish it.'

'Certainly! Now, let's hurry,' Holmes said. 'I fear if we outstay our welcome, one of these cutthroats might just take it upon themselves to try and stop us…'

Chapter Seven

'Follow the instructions written on the back carefully and do not deviate from them.'

I don't believe I'd ever packed my suitcases so fast. My clothes were squashed and poorly folded, but as I *was* staying at one of the most expensive hotels in the city of New York, I could have the laundry service fix the issue as soon as I returned.

When I was ready, I arrived downstairs and walked my cases to the concourse, where I met Holmes and Byrne next to a horse and cart. Once aboard, and headed away from Maximilian's Park of Amusements, I felt joyous.

'You should look for alternative employment,' Holmes suggested to Byrne. 'I expect once we have returned to New York, it won't be long before Maximillian closes his park.'

'All because of what he and Mr Russell were doing?'

Holmes nodded.

'You *knew* they were hiring convicts?' I asked.

Byrne sighed. 'They caused us no harm, sir. Most times, we never saw them. Occasionally you'd meet someone like Chip, but that was rare. He *was* nice though. Different from the others. Newer too.' Byrne then turned to us. 'Mr Russell ran, I heard. Took five thousand dollars from Mr Maximillian's safe, a few of the men, and he's gone.'

'I am not surprised to hear that. It's unlikely we'll see him again. He has betrayed his master and stolen from him. I think *this* problem might just take care of itself. I am going to give you a business card,' Holmes said. 'It's for a very wealthy man called Henry Royce Greene.'

Young Byrne gasped. 'I know who *he* is, sir. Why would you give that to me?'

'Because you are a bright, intelligent young man who, with nurturing and education, will one day make an excellent engineer. Now, do you enjoy working on these rollercoasters?' Holmes asked.

'I do, sir. But there aren't too many around.'

'How much money do you earn a week working for Maximillian? Five dollars?'

The young Irishman showed no embarrassment. 'Three, because I have to pay rent.'

Sherlock Holmes opened his wallet and handed Russell two ten-dollar bills. 'Add this to the five from earlier. When you have taken us to the station, return to your family. Do you have access to a telegraph office?'

'Yes, there's one in town, sir.'

Holmes pulled out his notepad and pencil. 'As soon as you get home, have the operator wire your contact information to the Fifth Avenue Hotel, care of Sherlock Holmes.' He scribbled a note. 'In fact, you can simply give the telegrapher this note. They'll know what to do with it.'

'I will, sir. Thank you.'

Holmes nodded.

Byrne eyed him for a moment, then looked to the road. 'Could you please explain one thing, if it's not impossible to do?' Byrne asked.

Holmes chuckled. 'Nothing is ever *truly* impossible, Michael.'

'Then how *did* Chip disappear, sir? That I would really like to know.'

I wanted to know as well, but I knew Holmes wasn't ready to answer it. He'd been evasive each time the subject arose, but then I perceived the smile he offered Michael Byrne as he regarded him, and instantly knew I was wrong. 'The answer might appear elementary when the facts are explained. Chip exited the station along with everyone else.'

'But sir—'

Holmes put up a hand. 'Chip sat in his usual carriage. Something he'd done hundreds of times before. So regularly, in fact, he knew every turn of the track. Every bump and every nuance of that ride. Time, Michael. It all came down to time, and these,' he said, taking those envelopes from out of his pocket, spreading them across his knees.

'What are they, sir?'

'Little pieces of evidence, Michael. Snippets of life, if you prefer poetry. Some with context. Some without. Samples of hair. Fibres from clothing. Slivers of wood. Cigar ash, and samples of soil. These are the things needed to build a certain type of picture, and they *all* have something in common.'

'Chip?' Byrne asked.

Holmes nodded. 'You said Chip didn't appear to be himself, because he was looking down at his hands?'

'That's right. He seemed quite miserable.'

Holmes shook his head. 'He knew he was leaving. It is natural to feel some sadness, especially if you are comfortable and have made a friend. But you mistook his concentration for misery. He was looking at his feet. The reason you didn't see Chip again after the train departed the station is simply because, from the moment he'd entered the carriage, Chip began a transformation. I am typically sceptical of anyone whose description contains "bushy red beard and red hair to match," but those suspicions positively intensified when you told me he not only wore brightly coloured clothing but also had a height disadvantage, meaning the poor fellow couldn't help *but* be noticed.'

We each listened to his explanation in equal parts awe and incredulity.

'In the twenty-five seconds it took the train to pass through the tunnel,' Holmes said, 'Chip had removed his wig and false beard, shoving them into the overcoat he'd turned inside out. Something I believe he practiced. When you saw him looking down, he was, in fact, smashing off those slivers of wood he'd attached to his shoes in order to build them up. Chip walked right past you, and everyone else, and straight out of the park. And no one saw him do it. Genius.'

'That's too incredible to believe, sir. And here is the station.'

When we had our luggage, Holmes turned to Byrne. 'Go back to your family, and don't return to the park until you hear from me,' he said, quickly adding, 'and don't forget to send that telegram.'

We watched the cart head off, then turned to the station entrance.

'Was that all true about Chip?' I asked.

'As true as the facts are,' Holmes remarked. 'Chip left the train as I describe.'

'To escape those men?'

Holmes shook his head. 'They were long gone by the time we arrived. Those men had nothing to do with anything, they just came on a day *I* also came. Pure chance.'

I frowned, because if that were true, then… 'Chip was running from *us*?'

Sherlock Holmes gave me a huge smile. 'Isn't it gorgeous? Because nearly all the employees are villains, they assumed Chip ran from one of them. It didn't occur to any of them that Chip might have run from me. In the three hours it took for him to see us, hear us, and recognise us – he enacted his plan, and by the time we caught up at the roller coaster, he'd apparently vanished.'

'Does this Chip know who you are, then?'

'He certainly knew enough to recognise we represented some level of danger. Chip either knew us by sight, or someone had warned him. Given his reaction, I must assume he might also know *why* we came. That makes him connected. When I recognised that, I *knew* we'd exhausted all our avenues at the park. We're dealing with intelligence, Watson. We've interfered in a way that has brought us to the attention of the owner – a particularly ruthless man so I'm told – so we might expect some dangers as a result.'

'You think this Maximillian might come after us?'

'I do. These people have seen *some* of my capabilities in action, Watson. Their leaders will recognise the threat I embody now.' Holmes then nonchalantly checked his pocket watch. 'Well, as we have twenty minutes before our train, why don't we relax with a smoke?'

After what he'd just imparted, I doubted I could feel relaxed again.

* * *

Our journey back to New York was uneventful. The train arrived at the brightly lit terminal, and we disembarked. It was dark when the ferry finally docked at Pier Fourteen, but I felt happier back in the city again. We walked the length of the sporadically lit Liberty Street, out onto Broadway, where we picked up a streetcar. Around forty minutes later, tired and hungry, we arrived at the Fifth Avenue Hotel. Two bellhops attended us, collecting the luggage and taking it up to our rooms. Holmes then turned to me.

'If you're quick, Watson, you should still be able to get a hot meal from the dining room.'

'What about you?'

'I have several errands to run. I may not return until the morning. Please give this note to the next porter you see. He'll know what to do with it.'

This was not a surprise. 'Then I wish you good night.'

'Good night, Watson,' Holmes said, then took off at a brisk pace, crossing the vast street, where he merged into the darkness.

I entered the hotel, found a porter, and, as directed, handed him Holmes's note. Once he'd read it, he acknowledged receipt, and to my immense relief, also told me the evening chefs were perfectly willing to make me any meal I might choose.

I awoke Sunday morning far happier than I'd felt in days. The weather had warmed a little and once I'd taken care of my toilet, I came down to breakfast hoping to find Holmes, but ended up eating alone. As I was finishing up, Wiseman came and handed me a note. It was from Holmes.

Watson,

When you have finished breakfasting, I have a task for you. With this letter, you'll find a small map with a route marked out upon it. Follow the instructions written on the back carefully and do not deviate from them. When you reach the final destination, you will find a small bench. I shall meet you there.

SH.

The map was a small section of a much larger one, with a route laid out, as Holmes said. On the back was a set of very precise directions. Where I should go and what I should do when I got there. How long I should wait before heading to the second, then third, and so on.

The route took me around the houses to various buildings, including the splendid Grand Central Depot. Alongside I observed lines of horses and carts going back and forth, either loading or unloading freight for various stores and businesses across the vast city. It was noisy, and the smell of coal and manure was heavy in the air, but there was something majestic about it.

Once I'd located the position Holmes directed me to, I waited the ordered length of time. I absorbed as much details and culture as I could, spending most of my time observing various people going about their lives, completely unaware of me. The scale and size, the grandeur of it was simply breathtaking. New York was entirely different from London. Both are bustling cities, set against a background of steam, smoke, and industry, but there was something a little more exciting about New York. I suspect because it was all so... new. Grand Central Depot appeared the busiest part of the city I'd seen by far. New Yorkers, I soon discovered, did nothing small. I checked my pocket watch and recognised it was almost time to move onto the next location.

* * *

The map and directions took me east along Forty-Second Street. There I entered Reservoir Square Park, and sat on the third bench which gave a view of a building with a spire. There I was instructed to wait for ten minutes; this time I elected to smoke.

Over by a fence, I observed seven men in light attire, some jacketless, all holding golf clubs, engaged in deep conversation, a few eyes drifting towards a group of six young women with parasols who were slowly walking by. I hadn't sat there long when a rather shabbily dressed, dirty-looking clean-shaven fellow, with a frayed top hat and matching overcoat, unfolded a newspaper and began reading. Before long, he spoke. 'Doctor Watson?'

I turned to the fellow to answer, but without looking at me, he said, 'Don't look, Doctor. The less time we're seen talking, the better.'

'Who are you?'

'A friend of a friend.'

'I see,' I said, not feeling very reassured. 'And that friend is?'

'Daniel Wiseman,' the fellow said, flicking over another page. 'For Mr Holmes.'

'I understand. And you are?' I said, finishing my cigarette.

'Just a porter, sir. From the Bristol.'

'How did you know who I was?'

The young man chuckled. 'I've been keeping eyes on you

for a while, Doctor.'

'I suppose that's reassuring. Do you have a message for Mr Holmes?'

'Tell him the girl isn't anywhere Fifth to First, from Ninetieth to Seventieth Street.'

The young fellow folded up his newspaper and stood. 'Good morning, Doctor,' he said, then walked off.

I reread Holmes's instructions and checked my pocket watch. Twelve minutes had gone by, so I hastily got up and set off on the third and final leg of my interesting city hike. I'd just reached the path running beside the Croton Distributing Reservoir towards Fifth Avenue, when I came upon a fellow whose posture *instinctively* put me on the alert.

The fellow was a rough-looking man no older than thirty, with a huge moustache that hung over his top lip. It was clear I was his target, and without warning, he came at me with what looked like a short club. I dodged his murderous blow, landing a quick sideways strike to the back of his head with my cane. The fellow cried out, falling to one side, but remaining alert. I made no move to engage him whilst – without initially breaking eye contact – he checked his head and soon realised it was insignificant. His eyes then flicked to my right and before I knew what was happening, I was locked in a tight bearhug from behind. I kicked back at my attacker, all the while monitoring the fellow ahead of me. His head injury hadn't been bad enough to incapacitate him, and he made it to his feet. I threw my head back and felt pain as I connected with my assailant's face. It caused him to release me and from there I ducked away from both, using the time to brandish my revolver – signalling my intent to use it, if they did not disengage.

They both came at me, and I shot the first fellow in the thigh. He collapsed with a cry, and it stopped the other, the one I'd facially injured, dead in his tracks. He soon lifted his hands.

'Easy now,' the brute said, backing away. 'We just meant to

give you a warning. No need for violence.'

'Really?' I said, cocking my revolver and aiming it at his head. 'I believe this fellow attacked *me* first.'

'I'm sorry for it, but won't you let me give my brother help, sir?' he begged. 'He's really hurt.'

I hadn't intended to hurt him at all. I lowered my weapon and nodded. 'Of course.'

'He's gonna need a doctor, I reckon.'

'Then move aside,' I said, instinctively holstering my revolver in my pocket. '*I'm* a doctor.'

The fellow let me through and I quickly assessed the man's wound. My bullet had nicked the right quadriceps, grazing the vastus lateralis. It was a superficial wound. I recall thinking at the time that I wouldn't have expected such a fuss from someone so apparently dedicated to violence, but the more the fellow cried out in apparent agony, the more I wondered if I'd caused him a more significant injury than my observations had discovered. After I'd patched the wound with my handkerchief, and stemmed the *very* light bleeding, I heard movement behind me. I turned in time to witness a huge fist as it flew into the side of my head.

My world then went dark.

Chapter Eight

'Do you honestly believe he cares where that money comes from?'

When I came around, I found my sight blocked by a rather foul-smelling potato sack, which had been dumped over my head. My hands and feet were bound, and from the feel of things I was in the back of a waggon being driven Heaven knows where.

I tried to pay attention to their conversations as much as I could, but after a while my head began pounding, and I know I'd slipped in and out of consciousness for a good portion of that journey. I had no idea how long I'd been held captive in the back of that wagon, so when it trundled to a stop, I attempted to roll enough of the sack away from my face to be able to peek at where they'd taken me, but then I was lifted up and carried out of the wagon and dropped on my feet.

'Walk,' a youngish voice said. 'Or we'll carry you.'

'You'll do no such thing. I'll walk,' I replied, with as much dignity as I could muster. 'But *someone* will have to guide me.'

After several minutes of shuffling uncomfortably with my feet and hands shackled to a chain, my shoes hit solid ground that felt like pavement. I was then lifted up a set of stairs, walked through a doorway, and deposited onto what felt like a heavy rug. The next thing I knew, the sack was lifted and as my eyes adjusted, a red-faced walrus of a man wearing a tuxedo was staring at me through golden pince-nez balanced on the very end of his nose. He grunted quite distastefully between great puffs of his cigar and continued watching me. I remember thinking I should probably say something, but my head remained a source of disorientation.

The fellow didn't say anything for the longest time and then the man I'd injured earlier came beside him.

'What shall we do with him, Max?'

Now I knew who he was. Cornelius Maximillian. And he appeared as odious as Holmes had earlier described. 'Clean him up, see to his head, feed him, then bring him upstairs.' He then turned and strode away.

'How's the leg,' I asked, since the chap caring for me was the fellow I'd injured. He'd unshackled my hands and I rubbed my wrists in relief. The young man simply stared at me at first, his face contorted with a mixture of anger and hate, and then he relaxed, and I was startled by his transformation.

'I've had worse. Besides, none of them's been shot by an English doctor, I bet!' He grinned at me. Apparently, what I thought would be a rather awkward conversation, turned out to be far easier than expected. I tested my luck, since the fellow had almost changed personality.

'What's your name?'

'I'm not gonna tell you that,' the young man said, his accent with a slight Irish lilt to it. 'But if you want to call me something, call me Charley.'

Charley, I thought. Was *this* Chip? 'Tell me, Charley. Have you ever been to your boss's amusement park in Newark?'

'Max's place? Sure.'

'Recently?' I asked.

Charley nodded. 'Why so interested, anyway?'

'If I said *Michael* was sad, would that have any meaning for you?'

'It might. Depends on what knowing it'll get me.'
'I don't understand,' I said, truthfully. 'Get you?'
'Yeah, Doc. How much do I get?'
I understood. 'You want *me* to pay for the information?'
Charley laughed as he shook his head. 'You'll never have need of it anyway. Max isn't gonna let you go.'
'I'm sure I don't know *what* you mean,' I asked, as innocently as I could.
Charley chuckled but made no reply.

It was time to find a way to leave. I didn't expect I'd be able to incapacitate Charley a second time, not with violence...no, not with violence, I thought. With science. I turned to Charley and smiled.

'I know. But I would really like to take care of your wound before whatever happens next.'
'You feel bad because you shot me?'
'I do.' And I genuinely did.
He nodded and I smiled. 'The first thing we'll need to do it clean this wound. Let me see what they have in this medicine cabinet. It appears well stocked.' I selected the bottle I needed and the clean bandages and came along side Charley.
'This might smell a bit,' I said, emptying some of the liquid onto the bandage.
'What *is* that,' Charley asked me.
'It's liquid trichloromethane,' I replied, adding three small drops of the liquid to the rolled-up bandage, which I then pressed into his face. He struggled against me, hard. His bucking became so frenzied I wondered if I'd miscalculated the dose, but when his fight finally eased, then left entirely, I eased Charley into a prone position and waited till he had fully succumbed to the aesthetic effects. 'Commonly known as chloroform,' I murmured as I made sure his airway wasn't blocked.

I slipped both bandage and bottle into my pocket and looked through my sleeping friend's person for the key to unshackle my ankles, and in no time, I was free.

The basement hospital had one means of egress, and it required traversing a loud, creaking stair to get to. The door wasn't locked. I peeked out into a corridor, and saw no one. I had no idea which direction to take, so I flipped a coin and selected heads for left. It was tails.

The layout, I thought, was reminiscent of a hotel and I traversed the corridor to another door, which I carefully opened and slipped through. I found myself in a dimly lit wood-panelled room with a small fire in a grate, the light of which was too weak to penetrate in the rest of the room, leaving most of it in darkness. The door behind closed, and when I turned, I could no longer discern where it had been. There appeared no breaks in the panelling. Despite several minutes of scrabbling around the edges with my fingertips, it remained maddeningly shut tight. The sound of a match flare startled me and I turned in its direction. Sitting in a darkened corner, now illuminated by the match flame, was Maximillian.

When he'd caught his cigar alight, he gestured to a chair opposite him. 'Sit, Doctor,' he said, his demeanour pleasant enough. I walked to the chair and found him pointing my revolver at me.

'Empty your pockets please.'

I did as he asked, and he pointed the revolver to the table. 'We had chloroform?'

'Yes, I was surprised to find it too. I used just a little on Chip,' I said, hoping the use of that name might illicit a response. If he recognised it, or understood its meaning, he didn't show it.

'Chip?'

'The fellow I shot earlier.'

Maximillian smiled, then turned his eye to my old service revolver. 'With a Beaumont-Adams, forty-five calibre. It's heavier than I thought it'd be,' he remarked, testing its weight. 'You're not like any doctor I've seen.'

'In what way am I different?'

Maximillian shrugged. 'None of the fellows I know would

brain then shoot someone. Seems like that's a betrayal of your oath to do no harm, or is that more like a suggestion in England?'

'That oath doesn't apply when in defence of myself,' I replied.

'And that includes drugging someone against their will with chloroform?'

'The concept of a solider *and* doctor hasn't reached the Americas yet then?' I asked, knowing of course it had. This fellow was being obtuse for a reason, and I was not long finding out what. Maximillian went back to testing my revolver.

'You fought a war with this weapon?'

'Several,' I answered. Maximillian nodded, then turned the weapon over to me. I took it with a mixture of elation and suspicion. When I checked the breach, he laughed. It was empty so I closed it.

'I wasn't going to leave it loaded now, was I?' the hefty man said with a chuckle.

I was tiring of his banter. 'Why have you abducted me?'

'Because you and your meddlesome friend have cost me, Doctor. I'm a pretty reasonable man, most days. You do something that loses me money, you find a way to get it back quickly. I've no problem stepping on a man's head while he's drowning. People need to know what happens if you disappoint me.' The door opened in the wooden wall, and Charlie and another man stepped in, caps in their hands. Charlie's eyes glaring at me accusingly. I looked between them.

Maximillian then said, 'It's going to take time to fix the problems you've caused. In the meantime, I have to decide how to deal with your friend. He's clearly a little more resilient than you, since my men have failed to bring him to me, but they will. Now, a trained doctor I *can* use. So, you'll work for me, until I say otherwise.'

'I'll do no such thing. You can't coerce me,' I growled.

'I can't?'

The odious Maximillian made a quick gesture, and the fellow behind Charley dropped a sack over his head. Before either of us could react, Charley's muted cries went with him as he was dragged from the room.

'Don't you *dare* hurt him,' I yelled, standing.

'Sit *down*, Doctor.' His expression was cold. I slowly sat. 'These are my people, Doctor Watson. They're mine to do with as I please. If you're a *good* boy, he'll be fine.'

'Do as I say, or Charlie will pay, is that it?'

I sighed at the terrible fix I'd found myself in. All the time wondering where Holmes was.

'You're a quick study I see. Well, you're a doctor, aren't you? But so we're clear. If you don't want Charley to be washed up on the banks of the Hudson, then you will do as I tell you to.' He took another puff on his cigar. 'I'm not unreasonable. I'll give you time to consider your position, you might even make a counter proposal of your own.'

I remained quiet. A part of my brain recognised the peril I was in and despair from that began to creep across my mind, but then another told me Holmes would know where I was. That porter I met earlier knew me, so I reasoned he'd probably report seeing me to either Wiseman or Holmes at some point, especially once I was declared missing. Holmes had contacts in New York as well. I pushed away those creeping doubts and remained impassive. I was sure if anyone could have found me it *would* be Holmes, but in order to be found, I'd need to stay alive first.

As if reading my mind, Maximillian said, 'This friend of yours, Holmes. Is he as clever as people say?'

'He certainly is that,' I responded confidently

'Good,' the fat crime boss said with a grotesque smile. 'I do like a challenging opponent. If you say no, I'll have to consider how to deal with you. You're hoping he'll come and rescue you, is that it?'

'I know he will,' I said, with a strength of feeling I truly felt.

'I'm sorry to tell you this, but...he's dead.'

I laughed. 'You'll never convince me of that,' I said. 'You'd do well to also remember we are friends with Mr Henry Royce Greene,' I added, hoping it might change the situation.

Maximillian just laughed. 'Nice try, but if Henry Royce Greene has a true friend in the world, it would be his bank manager. Greene has run more people out of this city than I have, and that's saying something. He's rich beyond many, Doctor, and that money buys him anything he wants. For a man to become as wealthy as Greene is, he needs to break a few backs to do it. Do you honestly believe he cares *where* that money comes from?'

'Well, you haven't killed me, so I don't believe you've killed Holmes.'

'I didn't kill him, Doctor. You did.' He threw something metal at me. When I caught it, my breath stuck in my chest. It was Holmes's cigarette case, and it had a hole right threw it.

'Where did you get this?'

The next thing I knew, and to my utter bewilderment, a hand clamped over my mouth. I had no idea anyone was in the room behind me. The last thing I saw, before I fell into oblivion, was Maximillian smiling, as he puffed away on that obnoxious cigar.

* * *

My eyes adjusted to the gloom of the room, and I blinked a few times. I was laid on a bed in a room that looked halfway decent. I threw my legs over the side and sat up, rubbing my eyes. I took a few deep breaths to clear my head. When I turned my eyes around the room, I was surprised to discover a quiet, rough-looking lanky man who was leant against a wall smoking. His dress was consistent with a style I'd seen common amongst the poorer people in the city. His hat and jacket were both frayed in several places, and his cuffs and collar appeared standard button-on. What caused me the most concern was the redness of his knuckles. It suggesting he'd fought someone as recently as that day.

The fellow hardly blinked. In fact, between his overgrown moustache and large cloth cap, there was hardly any face at all, and what you could see was dirty. Those eyes, however, had an intensity about them. As he stared at me the only word that came to mind was *menacing*.

'Here to make sure I don't escape?' I asked. The fellow pulled the cigarette from his lips, twisted it in his dirty fingers, and displayed yellow teeth as he exhaled, offering me a crooked smile before the smoke went back.

'Might I have one of those?' I asked. There was a sadness in the pit of my stomach. Could Holmes really have been killed? I just wouldn't believe it. Not until there was irrefutable proof. I struck the idea from my mind. While I began contemplating other things, the fellow reached into his pocket and threw me a pack, and the matches. I gratefully lit a cigarette and exhaled and then stood to hand them back.

'Keep 'em, Doc.' His accent was softer than the other New Yorkers I'd met.

'Thank you.'

I sat for some time thinking about Holmes whilst the fellow just stared at me, all the time just slowly smoking his cigarette. When he finished, he dropped it, put it out with his boot, then immediately opened a fresh pack and lit another. He pushed himself off the wall and came over to the bed. I eyed him uncomfortably as he fell against the wall beside me.

'You must have done something terrible to be put in here with me,' he said. He narrowed his eyes as if he was scrutinizing me. 'Or perhaps Max thinks someone is coming to rescue you?'

'He doesn't tell you these things then?' I asked flippantly.

'He don't have to. He pays me.'

'And what does he pay you to do, hmm?'

Again, that crooked smile appeared. 'I wouldn't want to turn your stomach. We're having a nice talk.'

I nodded. 'Another cutthroat mercenary, eh?'

'Not always. *Only* if that's the job! I cut throats when they *need* cutting.' The simplicity of his point of view appeared both amusing and terrifying. 'But apparently I'm not to cut yours.'

'Well, that's a relief,' I said.

'Max likes to play games. He's like a cat who has a mouse. Sometimes he eats it, and sometimes he just kills it for fun.'

'And other times he lets the mouse go?'

The fellow chuckled. 'That would be a nicer end, wouldn't it?'

'Do you have a name?'

'I do. But I shan't share it.'

I nodded. 'And you're what? My jailer?'

The fellow shook his head. 'Like I said. Max likes his games. Here,' he said, reaching into his pocket. 'Open your hand.' I obeyed, since it appeared foolish to provoke a man who cuts throats for pay. To my complete surprise he dropped five rounds into my palm, then he stepped away and leant against the wall.

I checked my jacket and found my revolver in the pocket. The fellow nodded as I pulled it out.

'Why would you give me this, when I could kill you to escape?'

'You could, Doctor,' the fellow agreed. 'But then you'd have four shots, and everyone in the building will know where you are.'

'I see. Then why?'

'Because Max likes—'

'To play games, yes I heard you.'

The fellow stubbed his cigarette onto his boot, then lit another. He must get through several packets in a day, I thought.

'So, what happens now?'

'If I were you, I'd go out that door and go right.'

'And if I should simply remain here?'

The fellow smiled. 'Then you're gonna have to shoot me, because I'll not let you. You have to play the game if you want to win.'

'Win? There's a prize?'

'Surely the best of all,' he said, bending forwards a little. 'Your *life*?'

I stood and loaded my revolver. 'Then I intend to collect my prize.'

'Good. Now, go right,' he said, and some of his menacing demeanour vanished. His eyes appeared kind. 'Trust me,

Doctor,' he said, and for instinctual reason I knew to. 'Take the stairs down to the next landing, head right and stay straight until you come to a wall with two doors side by side. They're storage rooms, of sorts. Wait in the *right* one.'

'For what?'

'Someone to take you out.'

'Why are you helping me?' I asked; my confusion must have been evident on my face.

'I'm *not* helping you, Doctor,' he said gruffly. 'I'm helping *me*.'

After I'd checked the corridor, I turned right, just as my cutthroat benefactor suggested, and armed, I cautiously followed the corridor to another turn, ending in a door to a staircase. Now I was convinced I was in a hotel. I had yet to see any windows, so I was unable to determine where in the city I might be. The stairwell was empty as I peered over the banisters. I appeared to be on the third floor, so trod carefully on the carpeted steps and made it uneventfully to the next landing. I followed those instructions again, seeing no one as I went, and reached the two doors, opening the right and concealed myself inside.

I had waited no longer than five minutes, when the door opened and the same fellow who'd given me those instructions appeared and gestured for me to follow. He took me around a number of corridors until we reached another door, which he then opened and ushered me inside. The room appeared to be a large, poorly lit dining-room or something similar.

The fellow then bolted the door firmly and from within the gloom came a compatriot looking just as rough.

'I am *very* pleased to see you alive, Watson,' the heavily disguised Sherlock Holmes said.

Chapter Nine

'You plan to turn them against each other?'

'Are you hurt?' Holmes asked as he checked me for injuries. The man I'd come in with remained at the door. I assumed they were working together.

'I'm fine, Holmes. I am glad to see you alive too.'

'A thousand apologies, my dear friend. My attempts to keep you safe were outdone by Maximillian's intelligence. He's a formidable opponent, Watson.'

'It was shortly after you directed me to that park. I met a young porter from the Bristol. He told me to tell you they'd not seen Jenny Fifth to First, Ninetieth to Seventieth Street. Shortly after, I was surprised by two men who eventually captured me and brought me here, wherever here is.'

'We're in an old hotel owned by Maximillian on Eighth Avenue. It's the perfect place to hide a criminal empire within. Hardly any villains in London have access to such wealth, thankfully.'

'The layout suggested a hotel to me, but as I had seen no windows, I couldn't really tell where.'

'That porter you mentioned,' the fellow at the door said.

'*Was* from the Bristol, but he's in Maximillian's employ.'

Holmes nodded. 'I failed to recognise that this network I had rather smugly appropriated for my use was, in fact, using me. You see, *some* members are part of a *highly* dangerous gang referred to as the Whyos, whose *modus operandi* appears to comprise anything from petty thuggery to murder for hire.' Holmes indicated to the fellow who had rescued me. 'This is Mr Stevenson, a Pinkerton detective.'

'Hello, Doctor,' Stevenson said. 'Mr Holmes isn't exaggerating about the Whyos gang. One of their former leaders, McGloin, had his boys running extortion, prostitution, and, as Mr Holmes rightly said, murder for hire.'

'They hanged this McGloin in the Tombs after he'd been found guilty of murdering a Hell's Kitchen tavern owner,' Holmes added.

Stevenson nodded. 'Louis Hanier, was his name. A respectable business owner. Gunned down in his nightclothes. We tried a few others alongside. Mostly petty criminals. These men aren't usually without a leader for long.'

'The Tombs?' I asked.

'The New York Halls of Justice and House of Detention,' Holmes answered.

Stevenson nodded. 'It's apparently modelled on an old Egyptian tomb.'

'Hence the name,' Holmes added.

Stevenson lit a cigarette. It was the longest time I'd seen him without one. 'I've been investigating Maximillian and his friendships with the Whyos leadership for some time. When the disruption of his organisation in New Jersey came to light, it caused a stir here in New York. Suddenly, there was a new name being spoken in these halls. It was a name I knew. Sherlock Holmes. Apparently, the Whyos and Max made significant financial losses when Russell took off with most of the money and men. He didn't come back to New York, though.'

'So, is Russell preparing to set up his own criminal enterprise, then?' I asked.

'We suspect so,' Holmes replied. 'The lost revenue from the park alone hurts Maximillian.'

'And Max won't stop till he finds Russell,' Stevenson said. 'Losing five thousand has got to hurt.' He finished his cigarette and immediately replaced it. 'I've admired and followed Mr Holmes's career for some time now. We worked a case in Ireland together. His superior skill assured our success, and he rightly deserved any credit for its solution, even though the Irish police felt otherwise.'

'I have not heard of this?' I said, turning to Holmes.

'It was before your time. And Stevenson is being *far* too modest. He is a gifted investigator. He found you before I did.'

'I had the advantage. I was already on the inside. But you did well to get as far along as you did, given the time you've been here.'

'What's happening in the park?' I asked.

'We've people there now, but we don't expect we'll find many answers quickly. Russell did a good job of burning almost anything of useful value. Almost the entire staff are gone.'

'How long have I been here then?' I asked.

'A day,' the Pinkerton said.

'That can't be right, it's Sunday afternoon.'

'You were out from the chloroform for several hours. It's *Monday*. One of my men sent me a message after witnessing your abduction. I knew where they'd likely take you, if you were still alive. I then had Mr Holmes picked up as we'd been keeping track of you both ever since you arrived.'

Unlikely, I thought. It struck me that Sherlock Holmes would only allow himself to be seen, if he recognised those watching weren't a threat.

'I have men in the Port of Entry, Mr Holmes,' he added by way of explanation. 'You're too important to ignore.'

'And I am grateful,' I said.

'As am I,' Holmes added.

'What I don't understand,' Stevenson said, 'was how you knew about this place at all, Mr Holmes? It took us a year to find it.'

'I began by assessing the fellow, and deciding what kind of criminal leader he was. It occurred to me this man liked everything close. His lifestyle, I saw, was one of opulence and extravagance. He wooed the very wealthy, often charming them into investing in his various enterprises.

'Maximillian's organisation is large. I rather suspected, given what I'd observed of the fellow, he'd want his minions close. He was rich, but not rich enough to own a building on Fifth Avenue. The first time we met, he was staying in a hotel on Fourth. I revisited it in my true persona and discovered it closed. A group of nearby workers then told me it had been closed for over a year. The owner, they'd said, had gone abroad.'

Holmes and I shared a match as we lit a cigarette each.

'I then went back to my list of investors. I highlighted any with a connection to this or any other hotel. That made the list smaller. I considered if Maximillian owned a hotel, then he'd need suppliers for food, laundry, guest amenities, such as toiletries and wash cloths and towels and so on – all in large quantities. Unsurprisingly, the richest people in New York all appear to visit the same stores. It wasn't difficult to bribe an employee into giving me a list of any of their clients who met those criteria. With this, I'd whittled my list down to five likely locations. I went to each. This was the fourth.'

'Amazing,' Stevenson said. 'We didn't think about trying to find his suppliers.'

'These fellows don't think they'll leave any trails or clues one might follow back to them. It really wasn't difficult to do.'

'So, how do we arrest him then?' I asked.

Stevenson laughed. 'You're mad, man! There's no way we can do that and survive long enough to take him to trial. Trust me, the Whyos will probably murder some of us before then.'

I turned to Holmes, who simply smiled.

'Not necessarily,' my friend said. 'I have a plan. In fact, Watson has entered right in the middle of it.'

'A plan of madness,' Stevenson said, chuckling.

'Possibly,' Holmes agreed. 'But you agreed?'

'Indeed,' Stevenson acknowledged.

I sighed. 'Well, if we aren't going to capture him, what are we going to do?'

'We have several newer problems in our way we must address before we even decide on that. The most urgent of which is finding a means of resolving the threats this gang poses to us, to Jenny, *and* the people of New York.'

'I still think it's risky,' Stevenson said.

'Will one of you please explain?'

Holmes nodded. 'Yes, sorry. My plan is to sour the relationship between Maximillian and the Whyos.'

I thought for a moment. 'You plan to turn them against each other?'

'No,' Holmes said. 'I plan to turn the Whyos against Maximillian. There's hardly any chance that we'll turn him, they supply almost all his muscle.'

'Meaning if they leave, he's alone?'

'Not totally,' Stevenson said. 'He's bought a lot of loyalty.'

'Yes, but the odds of being able to arrest him without causing a riot will be far better.'

'That is true.'

'He'll be vulnerable, and a *lot* more willing to talk. Imagine what he might give you? *Who* he could give you?'

'I'm imagining it, Holmes. That's why I'm letting you do it, even though you haven't explained how you're going to do it.'

'One step at a time.'

I was confused. 'Aren't these Whyos the gang who've abducted Jenny?'

Holmes said, 'I thought so, initially. Do you recall the moment Jenny was abducted? They cleverly assaulted our senses with reflected sunlight and strange animalistic calls?'

'I do.' That was when I realised the connection. 'Oh! That "why-oh," chant,' I said. 'I see now. *That's* how they named their gang?'

Stevenson nodded. 'They've been around since the '60s, amalgamating and reforming as they've gone, absorbing smaller rival gangs. They practically dominate the Forth Ward,' he said. 'Right now, you're safer here than outside.'

'But you no longer believe they abducted Jenny?' I asked Holmes.

'We may have misread that situation. It is my understanding the Whyos may have assisted someone else in abducting her. I have yet to decide how best we might help her.'

'Is Jenny still alive?' I asked, my heart lifting when Holmes nodded.

'None of these fellows murdered her,' Stevenson said. 'They're braggers, Doctor. If they'd harmed her, I'd know.'

'That's *some* good news,' I said, relieved. 'But what about Henry Franke? We haven't found him yet, either.'

'Henry Franke is a different proposition entirely, Watson. We shall not easily find him.'

'Why is that?'

My friend smiled at me. 'Because he doesn't *want* to be found, and what's more, he's done everything he can *to* escape. I know of at least two instances now.'

'Two?' I said, frowning.

'When Jenny assisted him to disappear at his home, and when he escaped from that rollercoaster at Maximillian's Park.'

'Henry Frank was Charles Murphy?' I said, my bewilderment clear. '*How* do you know that?'

'We have never met Mr Franke,' Holmes said. 'But we *have* met his brother. Our client?'

'That's true. They might look similar, I suppose.'

'Almost identical,' Holmes said, smiling at me.

'They're twins?'

Holmes laughed. 'No, Watson. It was Henry Franke who came to our hotel pretending to be his brother. It was Henry Frank who we met at his brother's pharmacy.'

I laughed, despite myself. I was more confused now than ever. 'How do you know this?'

'Well, first of all, up until recently he'd worked as a manager at the hotel. He chose the chair opposite you for one reason only. It offered him a view of the bar from which no one would see him. I believe I commented on the significance of that at the time?'

'Yes, I recall that.'

Holmes finished his cigarette and flicked it into an empty grate. 'That story of how his brother had been annoying rich people in the hotel to the point they'd threatened him with arrest, came from Franke. None of it was true.'

Stevenson nodded. 'I checked. The police don't know anything of it. Including Franke's disappearance from his home.'

'Mrs Frank didn't call the police?'

Holmes shook his head. 'She thought it was another one of his "stunts," so Mr Swank told me. 'She'd only recognised the significance after receiving a telegram explaining why we wanted to come and when we followed it, she began to suspect her husband might not have been playing a stunt on her at all.'

'But actually was,' I said, shaking my head. 'So is *he* a member of this gang, then?'

'They've got people everywhere,' Stevenson said. 'It wouldn't surprise me.'

'I think it unlikely. I did not see through Franke's disguise at the pharmacy right off, well how could I have? Not all pharmacy owners are chemists. I had no cause to suspect him at that time. But... *had* I been an ideal reasoner, I should have deduced it from the complaint levied by the lady Franke was serving as we entered. A single link, Watson. That's all it should have taken.'

'You can't beat yourself up over it,' I said.

'I am not berating myself, just acknowledging that no matter how far along we think we've come, we still have a long way to go.'

'What did this Franke do to make you reconsider him later?' Stevenson asked.

'He filled her prescription incorrectly in front of her. Twice. So, either he was distracted or incompetent. I can usually tell when a person is falsely attending a duty they don't completely understand, but instead of examining *both* possibilities, I reasoned his lack of application was the result of emotional concern for his lost brother. He'd been trying for weeks to find him. No one was helping. He was under a warning of arrest. If anything might fray a nerve, I considered, wouldn't that be it?'

'It certainly would,' I agreed. 'What happened to his brother?'

'He's been in Colorado for almost a month, Watson.'

It was all beginning to make sense. 'Franke's wife said she hadn't seen him in over a month. The way she ended that sentence suggested it was because they had no love for each other. But it was simply a fact. She hadn't seen him, because–'

'He wasn't there to *be* seen.' Holmes beamed at me. 'That was what first made me suspect I was being manipulated. I discovered *Thomas* Franke's wife is from Colorado, and with the help of a telegraph operator, I was able to review copies of telegrams various people, including Henry Frank *and* his wife, sent to her over the past week. From them I discovered her father is sick. They are with him there and from what I understand, he is unlikely to live much longer.'

'The Franke's are a wealthy family. That's how Greene allowed his daughter to marry one of them,' Stevenson added.

'It was apparently Franke's *father* who started the family pharmacy business, which isn't insignificant in its operation. There's a Franke's Pharmacy in almost every major city. Naturally, his brother had keys to the one in New York, as in his brother's absence, he ensures the staff are taken care of as they should be. The store closed on the day we arrived, but Franke opened it once he knew he'd caught our attention.'

'So, what's his game?' I asked.

'The evidence would still suggest he's attempting to escape his wife – or his wife's family.'

'I know *Mrs* Franke,' Stevenson said. 'She'll do anything if she's crossed, including using the Whyos.'

Holmes nodded. 'So neither her husband, nor Jenny, is safe from her. That side of my case appears solid. He *is* attempting to escape his wife's influence, then, and I believe he used her connection to the Whyos to aid his abducting Jenny.'

'Why *would* he abduct her?' I asked.

'Several reasons come to mind, Watson,' Holmes said darkly. 'None of them are pleasant.'

'So, how did we end up in *this* predicament with Maximillian?'

Holmes was thoughtful. 'Maximillian and Franke's paths appear to have crossed several times. Too many to think it's a coincidence.'

'Which *you* don't believe in,' I pointed out. 'Do you know where Franke is now?'

'No. I believe when Russell absconded from New Jersey, Franke returned to New York. He's somewhere here, Watson, but his location remains a secondary concern, for now. We *must* deal with Maximillian and his associates first. Once we accomplish that, our friend here has agreed to help us find Franke and rescue Jenny.'

Chapter Ten

'Why would I lie to you, of all people?'

'So, talk me through this insane plan of yours one more time,' Stevenson said. I admit, after hearing it, I felt the word *insane* had been awfully well chosen.

'It's simple.' Holmes checked his pocket watch. 'In five minutes, Maximillian will take his regular walk on the roof, where he'll smoke a cigar and watch the city.'

'Stevenson, *you* will engage the Whyos in the building and plant the seeds of discontent. What if Maximillian had *lied* about the five thousand dollars Russell had taken? The Whyos are proud. One of their own absconded with a client's money. They'll naturally want to make restitution, if they're to keep the alliance between them strong. If Maximillian is lying, how long will it be before revenues from their businesses with him dry up?'

'They'll want proof of these claims. That's if they don't just kill me for suggesting them.'

'You know where there's proof. Stick to our plan. You were in a meeting in Maximillian's office. You saw a telegram on his desk which ordered his men to do the "big job" on Russell.'

Stevenson nodded. 'You believe these men who've murdered for each other will break their pact over money?'

'I believe five thousand dollars is a significant sum. In paranoid gang members who expect others to cheat and lie as they do? It will turn them, yes.'

'Just so *I'm* clear,' I said. 'Where did you get all that money?'

'From Mr Greene. If you recall, I asked Michael to send a telegram for me. I realised he'd arrive at a telegraph office *before* I would, so I wrote my instructions and asked him to let the officer handle everything.'

'That's right, you did.'

'My telegram to Greene agreed to his request to find Franke and convince him never to return. I asked for five thousand dollars as payment, to be delivered to our hotel.'

'Good lord, and he just handed it over without questioning why?'

'Of course, Watson. That money, whilst tremendous in size to us, is a drop in the ocean to him. Men like Greene respect power and those who hold it. Men who command vast sums often expect others to do so as well. So, I reasoned, wasn't the "greatest detective in the world" *worth* five thousand dollars?'

'At the very least,' I agreed. 'But how did you know you'd need it?'

'I didn't. But when Michael suggested Russell had absconded with that amount, I considered it might be useful if *I* had the same. I believe there's a lesson in it for Mr Greene. Because as insignificant as that amount might seem in comparison to his entire wealth, these rich fellows believe every penny works for them.'

'And they don't stay rich by giving their money away,' I added.

'Exactly. So while Stevenson is seeding this eventual confrontation, Watson, you and I will break into Maximillian's office and put our evidence in plain sight. Then we'll leave it all up to the Gods.'

I frowned. 'You're joking?'

'Well, yes,' Holmes said, and chuckled. 'Are we ready?'

Stevenson extended his hand. 'Since I'll be dead soon, I'd like to say thanks for making it a quick way to go.'

They shook hands. Then Holmes said, 'Stay with the Whyos, but once this thing begins, when you can safely do so, I want you to head to Forty-Second Street. You'll find the New York Police Department waiting to assist you in arresting every one of them!'

* * *

The next hour went as Holmes had predicted. Most of the Whyos had left for various reasons, leaving a skeleton crew in the hotel. Stevenson had gone off to enact his part in the plan, while I followed Holmes as we made our way down to the ground floor, where Maximillian's rooms were located. Because their boss was on the roof, the bulk of his security had gone with him. When we arrived at the first door, Holmes quickly unlocked it and ushered me inside, then locked it again.

My friend rubbed his hands together and checked his pocket watch. 'We have twenty minutes before the villain comes down from the roof. Let us get to work.'

Holmes deposited a telegram under a pile of paperwork, leaving enough poking out so that it was visible to anyone looking for it. Once satisfied, he went to work on the safe. Holmes put a stethoscope to his ears, and slipped the diaphragm over the lock as if it were a heart. I knew when he was turning the dial, he was attempting to feel and hear the notches lining up on the series of interlocking wheels inside. He called it "manipulation," which he considered the purest form of safecracking. These are the things one learns when living with a consulting detective.

While Holmes was attempting to open the safe, I observed the room. It was as I recalled it from earlier, but I still could not see the door within the wooden panelling. I heard a snarl and Holmes spun the dial again and went back to work. I moved to the door we'd come through and listened.

My pocket watch told me fifteen minutes had gone by when I heard Holmes growl as he spun the dial for the seventh time. With my ear remaining to the door, I picked up an angry conversation, and it was approaching. I whispered a warning to Holmes, who was still turning the dial. His concentration was exact. There were beads of sweat on his forehead and top lip. Then, to my relief, I heard an audible click and his expression relaxed, as he opened the safe door, put the money inside, then closed and locked it.

'We're out of time,' I said, as the argument approached. 'We're trapped in here.'

Holmes shook his head and led me to a darkened corner where he pulled aside a decorative full-length curtain, revealing the door to a small closet we could hide in side by side. Inside, we discovered several spy holes, which we took full advantage of.

Maximillian burst through the door first, his bulk leading, a trail of smoke flowed from his cigar as six others followed close behind. Two were his security, that much was obvious. The other four were clearly Whyos. The front two figures who confronted Maximillian looked altogether hateful.

'Why would I lie to you, of all people?' Maximillian said, puffing furiously away. 'Russell ran off with *my* money. How'd you feel if things were reversed? What if I accused *you* of lying?'

'Seems to us there's an easy way to remedy the situation. Open the safe.'

'Or what?' the crime boss growled.

The fellow Maximillian was talking to seemed very agitated. I saw his hands flexing to fists as he talked. 'Are you refusing to open it?'

Holmes leant to my ear. 'Excellent, Watson. It appears the plan is working.'

'Of course not, but why should I?' Maximillian countered. 'If we've no trust, we've no business.'

The Whyos leader slipped some kind of device over his thumb. 'You'd better open it, or I swear—'

'Fine. If it will put an end to this, I'll open the—' He stopped dead and stared. 'Wait a minute, someone has been at my safe.'

'Someone? Who? You more like!' one of the Whyos shouted. 'He's making excuses.'

'No, I'm not.' I saw Maximillian run his eyes around the room. He knew something was off, but the cajoling from the gang members returned his attention back to them.

'All right! For Heaven's sake, I'll open it.' Maximillian pulled open the safe door. 'There! You see...' He's eyes widened. For the first time, I read fear in them.

'*I* see, all right,' the Whyos leaders said, pushing the bulbous Maximillian aside. 'I see what looks to be five thousand wrapped in amusement park flyers.'

The poor crime boss looked stunned. 'That *isn't* mine.'

'Well, whose is it then?'

'I don't know.'

'It's *your* safe, Max,' one said.

Another then gave a tremendous shout and grabbed something off the desk. 'Look! By God, if it's not a telegram *ordering* Russell dead.'

They all looked at Maximillian, who had now backed away, taking comfort nearer his men. 'Listen to me,' he said slowly. 'I didn't write any telegrams, and I did not put *that* money in my safe.'

'Then who wrote it, Max? And who else has access to your safe?'

'No one!' he growled, then frowned. 'Well, someone broke into it. It's that doctor. He did this!'

'He snuck in, broke into the safe, and left you five thousand? Who is he, Max, Robin Hood?' The Whyos men were laughing, but their leader wasn't. 'What's going on here, Max?' said the gang leader. The coldness of his voice was unmissable.

'They might murder him in front of us,' I whispered.

'It won't come to that,' Holmes breathed.

Cornelius Maximillian looked distinctly uncomfortable standing between them all. He crept his bulk closer to the larger of his men, a giant brute of a man, who stepped between his boss and the Whyos and looked ready to fight.

The tension in the room felt like it could ignite at any moment. Holmes remained deathly quiet as we both observed them. I could tell my friend was tense because he knew that any battle between these men might not *stop* at them. We could *all* end up being murdered. I felt my trusty revolver and knew at least I would stand my ground and fight with Holmes if it came to it.

Fortunately, it didn't, because a minute later we heard several whistles blown. All the heads in the room turned to the door, and Max used that distraction to grab a revolver from a side-table, which he levelled on the Whyos' leader. The fellow growled but made no moves to provoke him firing.

'It's the cops!' one shouted.

I felt Holmes move close to me. 'If they had any doubts then they're gone now,' he murmured.

'Traitor! You'll *pay*, Max. I swear it.'

'This has *nothing* to do with me. Why would I want to ruin my business?' His eyes narrowed, and he looked over at the door. The sounds of boots on the stairs were getting louder. The Whyos' leader said something and his men turned and fled. He turned to Maximillian.

'You'd better leave the city, Max. And don't ever come back. If you do, I'll skin you.'

'No, wait, I didn't do this!'

But he was telling it to an empty room, because when the leader left, Max's protection faltered. Soon after they too abandoned him. The sounds of violence we heard suggested they'd taken too long to make the choice, and then those men burst back *into* the room, with around fifteen uniformed police officers from New York's Police Department chasing. It was over – they gave up in short order and were hauled away.

Maximillian dropped his pistol, as two officers took him. Not long after, a lieutenant from the Twentieth Precinct arrived with Stevenson, who confronted Maximillian. The fellow's mouth dropped when his supposed best fighter picked up the discarded pistol and handed it to the police lieutenant.

'Hello Max,' the lieutenant said. 'I've been looking forward to this, for a *very* long time.' He turned to Stevenson. 'Bring him when you're ready.'

The Pinkerton agent inclined his head to the police chief, who nodded, then left the room.

'Betrayer!'

'You had a good run, Max,' Stevenson said. 'But it's over now.'

The fellow growled but said nothing, and that was when Holmes chose to reveal himself. Stevenson greeted him. Maximillian frowned. 'You? My vet from Detroit? *You* betrayed me too?' His look of anger soon mixed with shock as I also emerged into the room and stood next to Holmes. 'I knew I should have just killed you,' he shouted.

When Sherlock Holmes removed his disguise, Maximillian almost turned purple. The anger at seeing him was almost enough to allow him to break from the police officers holding him. 'You're dead!'

'As you can see, I am very much alive,' Holmes replied.

'I'll see you drowned for this. Franke! *Franke!*' Cornelius Maximillian yelled. 'I'll cut out your eyes if it's the last thing I do!'

* * *

With everyone gone – including the deranged crime boss, whose curses I felt I could still hear – we went to work gathering evidence. It seemed Max had never thrown away anything.

Stevenson chuckled. 'I think he kept a record of every activity, and a list of those he paid to do them.'

'One imagines,' Holmes said looking over at the Pinkerton, 'that these rats are all fleeing. I suspect we've dealt a blow to the Whyos gang, but not enough to end it.'

Whilst Holmes was busy with the files on Maximillian's

desk, Stevenson and I went through the safe. Holmes had rescued his money, which he said he intended to donate somewhere before we left for home.

'Here's something,' I said. 'A receipt book. Perhaps it'll hold a clue I'm unaware of?'

Holmes took it from me and began examining them. 'Good lord. Not only did Maximillian keep a record of all his transactions, but he also rather helpfully listed his suppliers too,' Holmes said.

'The same suppliers you'd already uncovered?' asked the lawman.

Holmes nodded. 'Plus a few others. There are big names on this... list.' He gave a start. 'I believe I have it.'

'What is it?'

'A purchase for three third-class tickets to Australia, via Liverpool, leaving... this evening at eight. Watson, this *has* to be for Franke. We must stop them boarding that ship.'

'Three tickets?' I asked.

'Possibly Maximillian's escape plan?' Stevenson suggested.

'This fellow is clever. If I read him correctly, I suspect he purchased three tickets to fool anyone looking for *two* passengers.'

'Where are they leaving from?' I asked.

Holmes turned the receipt over. 'There's no information here.'

'Australia? Wait a minute,' Stevenson picked up a shipping timetable from Maximillian's desk and began flicking through the pages. 'Here it is. The Kangaroo Line for Australia and New Zealand. Office One-Hundred Eight, Wall Street. They'll leave from Pier Ten on the East River. Our side.'

Sherlock Holmes nodded. 'Then we must hurry if we're to catch them *before* they board.'

The police were still searching the hotel when we finally emerged into the warmth of the late-afternoon.

'We might still make cocktails at Greene's, but only if we hurry,' I said.

Holmes turned a smirk on me. '*That* was yesterday,

Watson.'

'Oh.' I gave my best conciliatory look. 'I wonder if he'll ever forgive me?'

My friend laughed then pointed at the police carriage Stevenson had commandeered and pulled up beside us. We boarded and with a flick of the reigns, Stevenson drove us to the East River, where we stopped at the Wall Street Office of the Australian shipping line. We were soon shown through to a holding area where an enormous collection of people were waiting to board.

'We'll never find them in this crowd,' I said.

'Are they even in here?' Stevenson asked.

I frowned. 'I don't see them.'

Holmes remained calmly observing the crowd. His eyes scrutinising everyone. Eventually, his lips compressed and he pointed his cane to a shabbily dressed man in a heavy overcoat sat huddled between several other people. 'There,' he said.

* * *

'It's just a little *too* warm for a winter coat, don't you think?' Holmes said, as we confronted the man. The fellow turned to us, and despite his short hair, moustache, and glasses, it *was* Henry Franke.

'The game's up, Mr Franke. There's nowhere left for you to run.'

Henry Frank sighed. 'You're just a little too clever,' he said. 'Aren't you?'

'*Where* is Jenny?' Holmes demanded.

'I'm right here, Mr Holmes,' a girlish voice declared. We turned to find Jenny dressed as a boy.

Holmes's expression appeared relieved. 'You are unmolested?' he asked.

'I am,' Jenny said.

It was clear we'd got something wrong, and when Holmes's entire demeanour changed, I knew he'd put it together.

'We just needed one more day,' Franke said, putting his arm around Jenny. 'Just one more day.'

Holmes pointed to a shipping office where we took Henry Frank and Jenny. We then sat around a table. It seemed apparent to me now that Jenny may have gone willingly with Mr Franke.

* * * *

Sherlock Holmes lit his pipe and blew out the match. 'Throughout this case, I have made errors,' he said. 'But never was an error so better received than today.' He took a long pull on his pipe. 'It's clear to me now that you are father and daughter.'

Franke nodded. 'Jenny is mine, Mr Holmes. I met her mother, Ida, twenty years ago when I was just a boy and she was no older. Ida was a maid, sir, and we had a short friendship which ended when my father discovered us in the barn. She was sent away, but Ida kept in touch by writing to a friend and so I learnt of Jenny. Then one day Ida stopped writing, and after several tries, I discovered that the family she'd been put with had sent Ida to a convent where I learnt she had delivered the baby, but did not survive. For the next fourteen years, I wrote letters to Jenny and sent her money for schooling and food, and when she was old enough to write back, we made a plan. Things in my life had transformed. My father, who to this day cannot hide his revulsion when I am near him, forced me into a marriage with the most hateful woman I had ever known.'

Franke took a sip of the tea Stevenson had found us. 'You see, my father and Henry Greene were at school together. They'd been friends for years, but then there was a falling out over of a plot of land they both technically owned. It kept them apart for years. Well, my father decided early on that I was too reckless to have money *or* freedom, so he cut me off and told me if I wanted an inheritance, I would marry Greene's daughter. The union would bridge the gap and everyone would be happy including my father, briefly, who saw my acceptance as a sign I was coming to his way of thinking.'

'Everyone was happy, except for you?' Holmes asked.

Franke nodded glumly.

'*Mrs* Franke did not know Jenny's relationship to you?'

'God above, no! If she had, Jenny would be dead. The only reason I'm alive is because of what she gained from the union. A guaranteed stake in the Franke family fortune through our children. Except... she can't have any.'

'So, you took on your daughter as a maid, so you might be close together. And the morning you "disappeared" Maximillian secured you a place at his park?'

'Yes. Please tell me you have that man locked away somewhere?' Franke asked Stevenson.

'For a very long time, I suspect,' Stevenson acknowledged.

'Thanks to you, Mr Franke,' Holmes added. 'You crossed our paths quite deliberately and—'

'Before you go on,' Franke said. 'I'd like to ask that Jenny step outside. There are things she doesn't need to hear.' He turned to her. 'Wait for me outside, please.' Jenny then nodded and left. When the door closed, Franke turned to us. 'Look, I know what happens next. You'll send me back to my wife and we'll all make out like it was a joke. Except it *isn't* a joke. And Jenny *isn't* the punchline.'

'Agreed,' Holmes said, nodding. 'Why *did* you wish for me to investigate Maximillian?'

'Well, that's a long story. Max used to be my best friend. Then I discovered one of his biggest advances came from my father, who'd paid him to take Ida away. Later, I gained a friend in a nun at the convent. She'd come there for similar reasons some years earlier. She'd been teaching Jenny. Well, through her I learned Ida had *survived* childbirth. She'd apparently been taken by some men in the night and was never seen again. Ordered, I had no doubt, by my father. The description of one of them left me in no doubt who it was.'

Holmes nodded in understanding. 'When you saw I'd be attending the Statue of Liberty unveiling ceremony with Watson, you *meant* to put me in his path?'

'And that was *all* I meant to do, but you're a lot smarter than I realised.'

'We'd just seen you at your brother's pharmacy, and once we left, you went into action. You sent a telegram to your wife, telling her of our arrival. You followed us and hid on the grounds and waited. When Jenny came out, you sent a boy to talk with her. That was when you gave her the instructions for her to disappear.'

'That's accurate enough,' Franke said, his smile suggesting he was impressed.

'After receiving her instructions, Jenny led us into an ambush.'

Franke shook his head. 'No. She's entirely innocent in all of this. That *fake* ambush with Max's carriage... I set it up. Jenny had no idea why. She just followed the plan.'

Holmes smiled. 'And the Whyos gang handled the rest, using mirrors and their signature calls to disorientate us.'

'But just long enough for Jenny to get into her hiding place.'

'In plain sight, I suspect,' Holmes said.

'She was in the back of the carriage you'd retreated behind.'

Holmes nodded. 'Yes, and you did *it* well. I felt the probability Jenny was in Maximillian's carriage ranked higher, but by then I had lost her. I applaud you, sir.'

'After that, I headed to the park too and became Charles "Chip" Murphy.'

'A persona you built using the presumption of infidelity as a reason to explain your weeks away from your wife, so that you might wait out your time safely *before* returning to New York, where you'd both board a ship to Australia.'

'Yes, but *you* then arrived at the park. I hadn't considered it.'

'You should not have used Maximillian's carriage as part of Jenny's disappearance,' Holmes said. 'Had you not, it's possible I may not have *made* that connection to the park.'

Franke nodded. 'I underestimated you. Well, I thought you'd undo me, but I had my plan. Liam knew what to do if I gave him a certain signal. He hid Jenny while I enacted my disappearance. I then retrieved her and returned to New York.'

'You both intend to start a new life together in Australia?' I asked.

'That's it.'

'How did you convince Maximillian to purchase your tickets?'

'I confronted him over Ida. He lied about it, of course. Said he'd played a small part, and that he regretted it. We were young men then. I knew Max was an odious man, with more blood on his hands than even those Whyos knew about. When I asked him to buy the tickets, he agreed knowing what I knew would go with me, and I'd never be able to hurt him ever again.'

'You had him purchase *three* tickets,' I said, looking at Holmes. 'Did he intend to come with you?'

'No. I thought it might throw off someone who'd consider looking for *two* people travelling together.'

Holmes stood. 'As I suspected. Mr Franke, I salute you. Your skills and intelligence will certainly benefit you in Australia' –

Franke's eyes widened.

– 'and I think we've learnt all we needed to here. Incidentally, your first disappearance was a sloppy affair that a child could have seen through. Jenny should have had a better answer for why you dropped the mail tray.'

Franke laughed. 'But I *didn't* drop it. Jenny did. I'd just told her of my plan, and she was so joyous she dropped the tray. It caused me to make up something there and then. My original idea was far better, but when my odious wife come down the stairs, I had to think fast. Knowing how superstitious she can be, I just decided to vanish, there and then, and dropped my clothes on the spot.'

'And you then hid in the laundry basket,' finished Holmes. 'I traced it, but lost you.'

'I was out of that thing and off the cart before it got anywhere near its destination,' Franke said.

Sherlock Holmes regarded him with a smile. 'Then there was that second affair on the rollercoaster. The planning. The timing of it. How you used those slivers of wood to adjust and change your height. It was genius.'

'You *still* saw through it though,' Franke moaned. 'I did enjoy the thrill of that ride, and the time spent with Michael. He's is a decent lad. I hope he isn't in any trouble?'

'He is not. I've secured him a future with Greene's money. He certainly has the aptitude. It wouldn't surprise me if he ends up running his own park, someday.'

'I'm glad to hear that. Russell and the others aren't the worst thugs I've spent time with. I knew he intended to run if things got too hot. Are you going after him next?'

Holmes shook his head. 'I rather suspect that problem to take care of itself.'

'And was it you who suggested to Max that Holmes had been killed?' I asked.

Henry Franke shook his head. 'Not me.'

I frowned and turned to Stevenson, who also shook his head.

'Then who?' I asked Holmes.

My friend smiled. 'I did. It *had* to be a convincing message, and since I had determined the porters were no longer our friends, using their system – through you – I sent a message to Maximillan explaining Sherlock Holmes was dead, in Franke's name.'

'When we returned to the hotel?' I asked.

Holmes nodded. 'Exactly. I then left my cigarette case as evidence, which eventually got to the right person.'

'So, what happens now?' Franke asked. 'To me, I mean?'

'You must refer yourself to Mr Stevenson here,' Holmes answered. 'I am not a policeman and have no legal standing in your country.'

Stevenson turned to Holmes. 'The call is *yours* to make.' He turned to Franke. 'With your help, I have Whyos leaders and Cornelius Maximillian heading for the Tombs, where I hope they'll not return from. If it were up to me, I'd give you a medal.'

'Thank you,' Henry Franke said.

Holmes smiled. 'Then go. We have no desire to impede you, nor do we have any solid grounds to do so. You have committed no serious crimes as far as I am aware. It is clear your intention was always honourable. I say, go. Take your daughter and go enjoy a new life together in Australia.'

Holmes handed him a small leather attaché bag. Franke peeked inside then gasped.

'Mr Holmes!' he cried, tears filling his eyes. 'We will never forget this, sir.'

Sherlock Holmes tipped his hat to Henry Franke. 'Bon voyage,' he said.

Epilogue

Sherlock Holmes and I stood overlooking a huge parade from a window in the dining room of our Fifth Avenue hotel. We'd recently returned from Bedloe's Island where we'd watched the unveiling of the Statue of Liberty along with many dignitaries, including President Grover Cleveland who praised the Statue's promise of liberty.

An armada of ships, decorated in red, white, and blue, formed a naval parade to Bedloe's Island. They draped the French flag across the colossal statue's face and our anticipation for the official unveiling heightened. Even Holmes appeared in awe of the ceremony.

Frédéric-Auguste Bartholdi himself dropped the flag, but apparently in the middle of a speech by a senator, whose words were subsequently drowned out as cannons thundered, and brass bands roared. Steam whistles blew from hundreds of ships in the harbour, their salutes welcoming the Statue of Liberty to her new home.

Now in the comfort of a private lounge, we enjoyed the various processions of firefighters, soldiers, and veterans—including a regiment of American troops—who marched together down

Broadway to the sounds of many brass bands, and more cannons, and sirens.

'The hotels will be looking for replacement porters, if that police lieutenant has anything to say about it,' I said

'Some, perhaps. Many are innocent.'

'Wiseman?'

Holmes smiled. 'A more interesting situation. The fellow was deep in Maximillian's organisation.'

'What's going to happened to him?' I asked.

Holmes smiled. 'After he'd handed over enough evidence to solidly implicate several business leaders, I heard he got his wife to safety, with a little financial assistance from an unknown contributor. I suspect, just like Franke and Jenny, Wiseman and his family will also have earnt new starts in another city.'

'Imagine that. But will the police every think to look for him?'

'No. I made sure of that,' Holmes said.

Mr Stevenson, the Pinkerton agent, came and stood beside us. Holmes smiled at him. 'What's next for you, Stevenson?'

'It appears my time in New York has ended.'

Holmes nodded. 'Yes, I wondered if this exposure would force you away.'

'I have the pick of assignments, Mr Holmes. I haven't decided yet. Maybe I'll hitch a ride back to England with you? I haven't seen much of it.'

'And you'll be welcome, if you chose to do so,' I added.

'There he is. The man of the hour!' said the rather brash Mr Greene as he met us at the window. Stevenson, I noted, was also adept at disappearing.

'You appear happy, Mr Greene,' I said.

'And rightly so. You've done a grand service. I cannot express my thanks enough.'

'Your daughter might disagree,' I pointed out.

'But she'll learn to live with it. And you, sir,' he said turning his eyes on Holmes. 'You've earned your fee, sir. There's *no* denying it. The greatest detective in world, didn't I say so?

Money like that can change a man's life. I've made you wealthy, Mr Holmes. I think it's fair I get to know *what* you plan to do with?'

My friend simply chuckled. 'I've never cherished money, sir. I have simple needs and hardly anything beyond the essentials of life. A new pipe. A new microscope. Perhaps a new pair of walking shoes? These things are enough. I took a little for my expenses and the rest I gave away.'

Henry Royce Greene's eyes widened so large I feared his eyeballs might actually drop out entirely. 'Gave it away? *Gave it away!* Who did you give five thousand dollars to!'

'No one special,' Holmes said, smiling. 'Just a lone rider trying to find his place in the world.'

Mr Greene then roared with laughter. It didn't appear to be a cheerful laugh. 'I think you're insane, but I guess it *was* yours to do with as you wanted.'

'The work is its own reward,' Holmes said.

'Is that a fact? Well, you've probably set this fella up for life.'

'Oh, I *do* hope so, Mr Greene,' said Sherlock Holmes.

THE END

* * * *

Coming CHRISTMAS 2023

The Watson Chronicles

SHERLOCK HOLMES

Four Calling Birds

A Christmas Anthology

Christopher D Abbott

This captivating anthology features four classic tales from the career of Sherlock Holmes, each set against the backdrop of Christmas. From a mysterious additional stocking that appeared during Christmas Eve night, to a seemingly impossible murder, follow Holmes and Watson as they unravel the most inexplicable mysteries.

Get ready to be transfixed and delighted by this collection of Holmes mysteries for Christmas...

Available for pre-order on Amazon

The Watson Chronicles

Christopher D. Abbott, Keith R.A. DeCandido, Michael Jan Friedman and Aaron Rosenberg team up to bring you another stunning collection of Sherlock Holmes adventures.

A pea-souper descending over London brings with it many villainous activities hidden deep within those thickly yellow-hazed streets, and for Sherlock Holmes and his faithful friend Dr. John Watson, it often provides cases to test the detective's intellectual prowess and his affinity for the unusual and bizarre.

Pull up a chair by the fire and prepare yourself as Abbott, DeCandido, Friedman, and Rosenberg present you with *more* cases…by candlelight.

Available on Amazon

"Rosenberg's tongue-in-cheek approach charms, creating an endearing, hirsute hero. Readers are sure to be entertained."
— Publishers Weekly

Small-Town Yeti, Big-City Problems

Peaceful, unassuming Wylie Kang—a Yeti with an appreciation for more *human* creature comforts—lives a quiet life in his self-built sanctuary on the outskirts of Embarrass, Minnesota. But when violent dreams disturb his peace, and a series of strange murders plague the area, a Hunter comes to town, nosing after Wylie's trail.

Fleeing pursuit, Wylie packs up his truck and heads for the Twin Cities, hoping to lose himself in the urban jungle, only to find a thriving supernatural community.

Just as he begins to settle in—with the help of some new-found friends—he discovers the bloodshed has followed... as has the Hunter.

Can Wylie catch the killer, before the Hunter catches him?

Available through all commercial booksellers

NEOPARADOXA
https://especbooks.square.site

About the Author

Christopher is a Reader's Favorite award-winning author of crime, fantasy, science-fiction, and horror.

Described by New York Times Bestseller Michael Jan Friedman as "an up-and-coming fantasy voice", and compared to Roger Zelazny's best work, Abbott's Songs of the Osirian series of works brings a bold re-telling of Ancient Egyptian mythology. Abbott presents a fresh view of deities we know, such as Horus, Osiris, and Anubis. He weaves the godlike magic through musical poetry, giving these wonderfully tragic and deeply flawed "gods" different perspective, all the while increasing their mysteriousness.

His Sherlock Holmes stories, published in the Watson Chronicles Series, have been recognised by readers and peers alike as faithfully authentic to the original Conan Doyle. In 2022, after publishing seven individual Watson Chronicle stories, Christopher teamed up with prolific authors Michael Jan Friedman and Aaron Rosenberg to add a collection of Holmes short stories to the series.

Christopher has published with Crazy8Press and written for major media outlets, including ScreenRant.

Info@cdanabbott.com
cdanabbott@gmail.com
and find him online at:
www.facebook.com/cdanabbott
www.twitter.com/cdanabbott
www.instagram.com/cdanabbott
and at his website:
cdanabbott.com

Original Mystery & Suspense

Join Dr. Straay as he investigates the mysterious murders of Sir Laurence Gregson, and Dr. Simon Chandrix, in these classic Agatha Christie-styled murder mystery stories

Available on Amazon

Sci-Fi - Horror

More To Fear Than Fear Itself

When a horde of towering creatures wreaks havoc on FDR's Washington D.C., no one–including the president–knows where they came from. A desperate group of survivors makes it to Fort Detrick, where they seek refuge from the devastation. They think they're safe there. After all, It's FDR's state-of-the-art maximum-security facility. But relief turns to horror, as they find they've locked themselves in with a more hideous threat than the one they left behind.

CRAZY 8 PRESS
crazy8press.com

The Watson Chronicles

At the end of his own birthday celebration, Major Peterson shocks his seven guests by leaving the party, going into his study, and apparently shooting himself.

Inspector Delaware discovers conflicting evidence, however, and calls for help from Sherlock Holmes. Upon their arrival, Holmes tells Watson he believes there's more to Peterson's death than the evidence might suggest. Still, the facts continue to show that Peterson committed suicide—until they discover something that changes everything...

Available on Amazon

The Watson Chronicles

Not all the myths of monsters lurking in the dark are just stories. When Doctor Watson first took rooms with Sherlock Holmes at 221b Baker Street, he found himself embroiled in a world of crime and intrigue he could barely comprehend.

One year on, Watson's now confident about assisting the detective, no matter how macabre the case might be. So when a young coalman from the Yorkshire Moors appears at their door, begging for help to locate his beloved sister who disappeared two days before under mysterious circumstances, Holmes and Watson can barely contain their excitement. But that enthusiasm soon turns to horror when Holmes uncovers the enigma of the tiger's claws—and places them both in the sights of a murderous madman...

Available on Amazon

The Watson Chronicles

Christopher D. Abbott, Michael Jan Friedman, and Aaron Rosenberg team up to bring you a stunning collection of four new Sherlock Holmes adventures.

From the cobbled streets of smog-filled London to the sweet country air of Scotland and beyond, Sherlock Holmes and his faithful friend Dr. John Watson embark on cases that test the detective's intellectual prowess, as well as his affinity for the unusual and the bizarre. Pull up a chair and prepare yourself to hear these cases . . . by candlelight.

Available on Amazon

Made in United States
Orlando, FL
10 January 2025